# Advance Praise for Ellen Meeropol's Sometimes An Island

"With acute vision and deep soulfulness, Ellen Meeropol imagines the fate of our fragile planet. In this powerful, prismatic novel-in-stories, she weaves a layered portrait of humanity's capacity for love—and for destruction."

— Debra Jo Immergut, author of *You Again*

"Told in a cascade of Greek chorus-like voices, *Sometimes an Island* is a chilling story of the world we live in and our precarious place in it."

— Ann Hood, author of *The Stolen Child*

"*Sometimes an Island* captures the peacefulness offered by the secluded island life of Penobscot Bay in Maine, while juxtaposing that simplicity with the many family tensions that define us all. Ellen Meeropol writes in a precise prose that imbues her characters and the locations in which they live with a beautiful clarity that rings true. As a resident of Vinalhaven Island, I found *Sometimes an Island* to be both authentic and a true pleasure to read."

— Caleb Mason, author of *Thickafog*

In *Sometimes an Island*, Ellen Meeropol weaves a miraculous story of love, loss, and resistance—braiding past and future in a haunting portrait of a family's multi-generational struggle on their coastal Maine island. As the climate crisis ravages the world in 2029, this saga of intentional communities transforms into an urgent warning and a radiant wonder. With precision and emotional depth, Meeropol illustrates how our connections to each other become our most vital resource against encroaching devastation. A masterfully crafted story that celebrates the fierce, fragile resilience of the human spirit when everything familiar threatens to wash away.

— Randy Susan Meyers, international bestselling author of *The Many Mothers of Ivy Puddingstone*

"Gorgeously written, this novel-in-stories brings the world—past and future—so alive you can taste, feel and see it. *Sometimes An Island* asks the question: can our stories save us? A family that once fled pogroms finds the answer as they grapple with impending disaster. Highly recommended."

— Rene Denfeld, bestselling author of *The Child Finder*

# Sometimes an Island

Copyright © 2026 by Ellen Meeropol
*Sometimes An Island*

Published 2026, by Sea Crow Press LLC
www.seacrowpress.com
Barnstable, MA 02630

Paperback ISBN: 978-1-961864-50-4
Epub ISBN: 978-1-961864-51-1
Library of Congress Control Number: 2025945589

All rights reserved.
No part of this book may be reproduced in any form or by any electronic or mechanical means, including information storage and retrieval systems, without written permission from the author, except for the use of brief quotations in a book review.

*This is a work of fiction. All characters, organizations, and events portrayed in this novel are either products of the author's imagination or are used fictitiously.*

*For Robby*

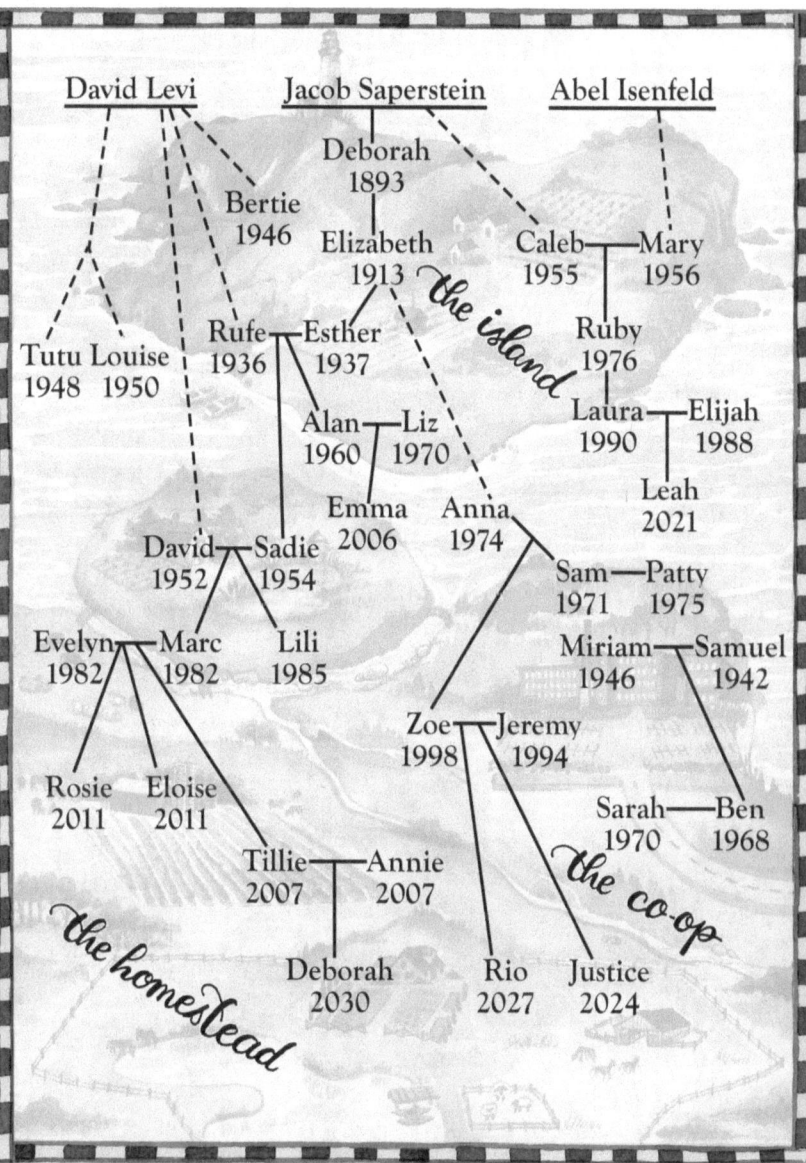

# Sometimes an Island

### Ellen Meeropol

Sea Crow Press

# Prologue

In the early years of the 20th century, pogroms against Jews escalate in the Pale of Settlement, the portion of the vast Russian empire where Jews are allowed to live.

After Cossacks attack their families and burn their homes, three young men and a girl escape from a shtetl near Odessa and settle on an island in Penobscot Bay, Maine.

Over a century later, some of their descendants flee rising sea levels to homestead in central Maine, calling themselves climate refugees.

They are joined by a cousin from Massachusetts and members of her co-op which split apart when a member was sent to prison as an eco-terrorist.

The island. The homestead. The co-op.
Three communities fleeing danger
Three intentional families facing the Great Undoing of 2029

# Drowning in Maine
## the homestead · 2022 · Sadie, Tillie, Evelyn

### Sadie

I am jittery, waiting for them to arrive. Which should be soon, assuming they remembered the map. "You won't have cell service once you leave town," I told Marc and Evelyn several times. Of course, once they get here, our worries aren't over. Can this place support all of us? Will the seven of us be able to stand each other?

David and I moved to rural Maine a year ago. I have questioned that decision every single day.

What will our son's family think about our little homestead? Will my granddaughters appreciate the four shelves of young adult novels on the floor-to-ceiling bookcases? Or the stacks of puzzles and board games? I run my fingers across the long pine table we lugged here from the island, feeling the scratches and gouges from generations of family meals and art projects and science fair experiments. There's room to feed all the kin I hope to gather here.

I sweep ashes from the hearth into the fireplace, then straighten the nesting matryoshka dolls lined up in descending size along the pine mantelpiece. They are our family totem, our legacy, rescued by my great-grandmother when she fled the Cossacks. On the dolls' stylized, painted faces, I superimpose the expressions of my grandchildren, five generations removed from the Pale of Settlement:

twins Rosie and Eloise, and their older sister Tillie. Why does the idea of these dear girls playing with the matryoshkas bother me? I could move them into my bedroom, but the nesting dolls have *always* lived on the family mantel, handed down from grandmother to granddaughter on her sixteenth birthday. My mother gave them to my niece Emma last spring, but Emma was off to college in California and asked me to hold them for her. I touch my index finger to my lips and then to the face of the smallest doll.

David and I grew up on an island in the middle of Penobscot Bay. On Saperstein Neck, often called Jew Neck because our kin settled there after fleeing hate in Russia. Is that nickname offensive? Probably, but after the violence they escaped, our ancestors shrugged it off and now we're used to it.

We're cousins, David and me, not unusual with the limited gene pool in places like ours. We always lived on the island, never even dreamed of leaving, though I wasn't surprised when our children moved away. Our quirky island house wasn't just our home; it was our history, built by my great-grandparents from blocks of the granite that drove the island economy back then. My grandparents brought it into the twentieth century with indoor plumbing and electricity. David and I raised our children in those drafty rooms and my elderly mother still lives there. I miss that house and the island—the slanted floors, the rocky coast, the low tide aroma, the quarries abandoned to swimming, the certainty of tides—like an amputated arm.

How could we leave our history behind? Because it became personal that global warming wasn't just another political cause: it was life-threatening and it was now. So we bought these twenty acres on the mainland, with plans to gather our family there sometime in the near future. Another fleeing, another migration.

Our family on the island refused to talk about the environment, despite reports of rising sea levels. For years, when I added the modern plague of climate change at our Seder, people responded with, "Can't we talk about something pleasant?"

When that 130-square mile chunk of Greenland's ice cap broke off in the northeast Arctic last year, I took it very personally. I'm no climate expert like my daughter-in-law Evelyn, but that much ice melting in the oceans translates into big trouble for people living on islands, or near the river like our Brooklyn family. Very soon, neither of those places will be sustainable. Our daughter lives with her wife and their kids in southern California; between the fires and the drought and rising oceans, they'll need rescuing too, though I don't think they will come. David and I decided it was time to heed the warning. We retired and moved inland.

When we returned home to sit Shiva for my father a few months ago, I invited our family to join us at the homestead. Cousin Tutu hated the idea. "Rufe would be terribly disappointed in you," she said, shaking her finger at me. "There are so few of us left, and your house is kin." Tutu is not clever, but her response made me pause.

I tried not to nag my mother about moving; Esther's heart had no space for anything other than losing Rufe. She says she understands about the climate crisis, that it will all come undone in the not-too-distant future, but she refuses to leave the island. She's old and grieving my father, wants to die in the house where she was born. The matryoshka dolls live here now, safe from flooding, but my mother still has our shared collection of wishing stones. She believes that rocks encircled with an uninterrupted white vein bring good luck, though there's not great evidence for that.

I miss her. I'm 68 years old, but when my nightmares come, no one can comfort me like my mama.

Maybe this latest ice chunk didn't drown us all, but the next one could, or the one after that. Or massive wildfires. Or drought. Or another grid failure like the one a few years ago. In any case, it galvanized us to leave our home and begin gathering our clan. We adore our family, every one of them, even Tillie, who is going through her less-than-mellow adolescence. I couldn't believe it when Marc and Evelyn agreed to join us, and so suddenly. I was so happy.

But can we live with them?

I guess we'll find out.

# Ellen Meeropol

## Tillie

The last thing I texted J before the signal died was this: *I'm being kidnapped. Call 911.*

No clue if it went through—not sure I even wanted it to—but what else could I do? I'm on some stupid two-lane road heading for Nowhere, Maine with my crazytown parents and deeply annoying twin sisters.

So maybe kidnapping is a minor exaggeration. Just one click below the actual crime. But only because it's my parents doing the deed. Taking me. Against my will. Against everything.

Can you believe no advance warning for this move? Well, almost none. Mom mentioned it a few months ago, but for later in the summer, after camp, and I told her no way and I thought everything was settled. Then the wildfires up north blew nasty air to the city and twin Rosie ended up in the hospital with an asthma flare. She was pretty sick, and the air is still in the red zone, but it's just asthma and Rosie came home yesterday with new inhalers and a nebulizer for when it's really hard to breathe. Anyway, Mom totally overreacted and last night at dinner, as we ate takeout sushi and celebrated the last day of school, she announced we were leaving at eight a.m. Today!

Is that legit? To forcibly take a 15-year-old Brooklyn girl away from all the people and places and things she loves? Right before J and I are supposed to head to summer camp, the best thing in my life? Telling me to pack one suitcase of clothes and one of books and art supplies and not to bother with screens, since there's no Internet where we're going, and crappy cell service too. They wouldn't talk about it, wouldn't reconsider, no matter how much I yelled at them. The car, that's another thing. Our sweet little beetle is gone, the car I planned to learn to drive next year. I won't be caught dead driving this butt-ugly beast.

I stare out the window, willing myself not to scream. Or cry.

Finally, sitting in the parking lot a.k.a. the BQE, Mom explained that the bad air and Rosie's asthma was the last straw and that our Brooklyn neighborhood will be underwater, and sooner than we think. Mom teaches high school science and considers herself a climate expert. Not that I don't believe her. I've been protesting fossil fuels since I was in diapers, first dragged by her and then going with friends in Extinction Rebellion and Sunrise. But instead of fighting to change things, instead of marching in the streets or blowing up pipelines or trashing the homes of fossil fuel executives, my mom runs away to the north woods and drags us with her.

Coward.

I'd rather breathe toxic air from wildfires or drown in raging swollen waters with J than be exiled with my family to dry land in Forgotten, Maine any day.

No matter what I want, we're fleeing to Maine. *Not* our rocky Maine island where Dad grew up and his family lived from the beginning of time, with its old-fashioned main street and icy ocean water and deep quarries. The island was boring, but at least it came with a rowdy tangle of cousins to be bored with. And not the cool Maine either, the coastal part with lighthouses and funky stores and rocks to jump on and lobster rolls. Mom says those beaches will be swamped by rising seas, just like Brooklyn. We're heading into wild inland Maine, home of moose and whitewater rivers, far away from J and everything else that matters.

This is my grandparents' fault. When the twins were born eleven years ago, my dad's parents finally figured out that Earth was doomed. Grandma Sadie denies that they just woke up. "We've known about global warming for decades," she boasted last Passover. "We attended the first-ever Earth Day in Ann Arbor. 1970."

Ha! It took them more than 50 years, but I guess they finally got it that climate disaster is here and now. They bought a homestead—that's what they call that dump—so that our family can survive the coming apocalypse off the grid with solar panels and growing our own food and everything. Last year they moved to moose central and started lobbying everyone to join them.

I've only seen their homestead once. Last summer, the grands persuaded us to take our vacation there instead of on the island. The land was hilly and rocky, the pond all murky, dark with weeds. Pretty enough if you like that kind of thing. The house is tiny. For vacation, we set up two tents in the yard and camped. But Maine winters? No way. My grandparents have the only bedroom, so Mom and Dad plan to winterize the screened porch, leaving me and the twins to share the loft. Really, it's an attic with a pointy ceiling and itty-bitty windows at either end. Mom promised we can partition the room, but even so, I figure I'll jump out a window by the second week. If I can manage to squeeze and slither through the tiny frame.

The grands started a small garden last summer. Enlarging and planting it is our first job. Mom says that the grid will probably fail so we can't rely on freezers or even refrigeration. Batteries for their solar panels are on the horizon, but in the meantime we'll can veggies. There's just one small detail—no one in our family knows how to grow anything edible. Eloise grew flowers in pots on the windowsill in Brooklyn, but you can't eat tiger lilies. Even I knew they were poisonous. Wait, she had those plants that trap flies, so maybe we'll steal their catch and become insectatarians.

As we drive, everyone is assigned critical topics to read up on and manage that crop. We'll visit the village library and take out books. Can you tell my parents are—were—both teachers? Eloise was assigned potatoes, Rosie got bees and honey. Grandma already manages the garden and Grandpa has his chickens. Dad claims the macho-man stuff, like fishing and hunting. Right. A college English professor. Maybe he'll recite poetry and charm the fish into his boat. Wait, he doesn't have a boat. And what does he know about fishing in a river, anyway? Aren't the fish different from the ocean?

My assignment is tomatoes. Growing them, harvesting them, canning them, making sauce—you name it.

We stopped to eat lunch at a pull-out along the Penobscot River. No facilities, the sign announced, but thick bushes to pee behind and flat rocks to sit on. There's been a lot of rain, Dad says, and the river was wild. Rosie wanted to swim but Mom said it's treacherous and people die every year on that river. I pondered tomatoes as I ate my sandwich and swatted at black flies. I've never really thought about tomatoes before.

After Mom's dinnertime announcement, I spent hours on the phone with J. Hardly got any sleep because I couldn't stop sobbing into Silverbutt's fur. That's another thing. We can't bring my cat with us. I argued like crazy that cats are great in the country because they eat mice, right? Mom wouldn't budge because Grandma doesn't like cats and they might be a trigger for Rosie's asthma. Personally, I'd rather have the cat. J stopped by just before we left this morning and took him, along with all his kitty stuff, promising to send photos. Mom said we'll go to the library in the village once a week and use their computers. Once a fucking week!

## Sometimes an Island

No phone. No iPad. No laptop. I brought them all anyway, because how could I not? Mom said we'll get used to a post-digital world, reading real books, using paper maps, and learning the pleasure of writing—and receiving—real letters. Like that's possible. Why not just give us a slide rule? Or an abacus? To add to the time warp, when we got into the car this morning Mom handed us each a small book with a lock and a tiny key on a leather strap. "You just write 'Dear Diary' and pour out your heart," she said, "and it's like writing to nobody and the whole world at the same time." She said she had a diary like these when she was growing up and it saved her life.

I look out the window at trees, trees, and more trees. No way a fucking diary can save mine.

### Evelyn

I'm the first to admit that we didn't think this out very well.

Marc and I have been talking for months about moving to his parents' land in Maine, probably at the end of August. We mentioned it to the kids but didn't push after Tillie's emphatic 'no fucking way' response. Still, we didn't renew the lease on our apartment and figured we'd move after summer camp, so we could all settle there before the new school year.

Then the Canadian wildfires went crazy and the air in Brooklyn —never great—became so toxic that my sweet Rosie ended up admitted to the hospital. They sent her home after three days, but said she had to stay inside until the air cleared. Inside? How could we manage that with jobs and everything? It was the last straw. Marc thinks I'm overreacting, as usual. He wants to wait. For another hospitalization, or worse? Like it will all go away if he ignores it? I raged and insisted and here we are, climate refugees heading north.

I hate that the kids will miss camp, not to mention losing all that tuition money. I hate springing this on them without warning. Most of all, I hate that Marc is furious with me, says I'm catastrophizing. I tried to tell him about the toxins in wildfire smoke, the benzene and formaldehyde and acrolein, worse than cigarettes, and they're everywhere with the fires. He doesn't want to hear it. He's going along, reluctantly, but he's barely talking to me. Just makes a bad situation worse.

With all this going on, it is hard to imagine anything less enjoyable than being in the car this morning with my silent and furious husband, our surly teenager, and the twins, one with her head stuck in a book and the other coughing. Then there's the car. I miss our little bug, so perfect for Brooklyn. Easy to park, cheap to fuel, but a squeeze for five people for more than five minutes and barely enough trunk space for a family of mice. The beast of an SUV Marc brought home yesterday offends me—why not a plug-in hybrid?—though I get that it's probably the right car for rural Maine. More than anyone, Marc mourns the bug, and he blames me for that too. He bought that car second-hand in college and painted it all psychedelic—my sweetheart was always decades out of date—and babied it along all these years. When he got the job at the college and the dean suggested a more dignified image, Marc switched to a student parking lot. Dignity was never his strong suit.

Tillie took one look at the new car and said, "That's ass." For those who don't hang with teenagers, that's not a compliment.

Driving north for hours, Marc steers the tank on twisty roads, while Eloise devours a decades-old edition of the *DeLorme Atlas and Gazetteer* and Rosie writes in her new diary, chewing on the end of her pencil between coughs. Tillie mutters to herself, no doubt damning us all to hell for taking her away from everything important in her world, especially J. I admit to being a bit relieved to get Tillie away from her—their—influence. I sit in the passenger seat with the map of our new home state on my lap, trying to find our position along the route marked in yellow highlighter. When was the last time I used a paper map?

"Where's the turn?" Marc can't keep the annoyance from his voice. "Do you want me to pull over and check the map?"

"Coming up soon," I say, but I'm thinking about our apartment in Brooklyn. My sister is probably there, packing our books to send to our new home and listing our furniture on Buy Nothing. By August the place must be ready for the next family to squeeze into 1000 square feet for an outrageous rent. Maine will be much more affordable. If we can find jobs.

While I study the squiggly lines, trying to concentrate, Eloise looks up from the *Gazetteer*. "Did you know our new town only had 1053 residents at the last census?"

"That's half the size of my school." Tillie's voice oozes disdain.

"It's an adventure," Eloise says mildly. She knows better than to engage Tillie.

"Slow down." I wave the map. "The turn is coming up. It's confusing because the road keeps changing its name."

Marc forces a laugh. "If you're confused, that means you don't live around here and they don't care if you get lost."

"Not very welcoming." My turn to hide the irritation in my voice.

"That's Maine."

"According to the *Gazetteer*," Eloise reads, "we'll be centrally located. Just a few hours to Bangor, to the ocean, to Canada."

*Brooklyn* is centrally located. I was born there, grew up there, have always lived there. In our early days, Marc argued we should move to the island, but no way. Our compromise was to spend a month every summer with his parents in the old stone house that has been in his family for generations.

"The river is famous for whitewater rafting." Eloise shows the map to her sisters. "That'll be fun."

Tillie slaps it away.

"Tillie." My reprimand is automatic and ignored.

Marc insisted on naming our firstborn after Tillie Olsen. I wasn't sure I wanted a verbal firebrand for our girl's namesake, but what do you expect from a professor specializing in $20^{th}$ century feminist short fiction? He says I should be grateful he didn't lobby for Flannery or Grace. Tillie is cranky in the best of times, and this isn't the best, for any of us.

"Here's the road," I say with more pride than justified.

As Marc makes the turn, I note the tension in his jaw. We argued about taking the kids from city schools after they lost so much with the pandemic. Rural schools were good enough for him, Marc insisted. Got him a good teaching job, which he has now left behind, thanks to me being a drama queen.

After about ten miles, the road turns to gravel. From the directions Sadie sent, there are twenty-seven miles of this. The jouncing is bad enough that Eloise puts down the *Gazetteer* and covers her mouth with her hand.

Tillie pinches her sister's arm. "Don't you dare barf."

"She can't help it," Rosie says.

Tillie smacks Rosie's shoulder. "You shut up! This is all your fault."

What have I done?

## Tillie

Dear J,

Don't laugh.

We got here yesterday afternoon, 24 hours, but I'm already desperate. Otherwise, I wouldn't be caught dead writing a letter. On a piece of paper. Can you believe I'll put it in a banged-up old mailbox at the side of the road, put up the red flag, and the letter carrier will pick it up like pony express? A carrier pigeon would be quicker.

I'm sitting in my third of our attic room, which is separated from the twins' section by a bed sheet hanging from cobweb-decorated ceiling beams. The sheet has faded pink posies on it, but this is no garden. My bed is tucked under the eaves, a real head-banger. On my pillow, someone left an odd dog figure made from reddish clay. A terrier, I think, with droopy ears, a broken tail, and a sad expression. Grandma probably left it for me because she knows how much I miss my cat, but this is a pathetic substitute.

I spent all day in the garden with Grandma and the twins, preparing the dirt for planting. Mom, who routinely killed every green thing she brought into our apartment, is lecturing Grandma about permaculture. She says it's as old as the stars and as new as TikTok, which made me laugh because she's an expert on social media? Like organic on steroids, she claims, except no chemicals so the steroids analogy is bogus. None of that matters because Grandma has had a garden every year since she was born, and Mom grew up in Brooklyn and knows nothing about growing stuff to eat, except what she teaches in her stupid biology classes. Taught.

When my blisters started bleeding (okay, I might have picked at them), I got permission to come inside.

The evil twins are still in the garden, happily arguing about how far apart to drop the spinach seeds and how deep, so I have this space to myself. Garretts are supposed to be charming and full of literary angst and promise, but this one is just hot. There's no air. Mice or bats scratch and scurry in the walls.

J, this is as bad as I thought it would be. We're totally cut off from the world. How can people live this way? Maybe it's worse than I thought. Apparently, we're only Phase 1 of my grandmother's plan to save the world. Once we've "settled in," as Grandma put it last night, we'll talk about how to gather the rest of the family. A glorious commune, she says. A shitshow, I say. My Aunt Lili is cool, and her wife loves to dance on the beach—and I mean really dance, wild and crazy and fun—and their kids are okay, but there's no beach here and they're so fucking California, you know?

Here's the thing: I'm going to die if I can't talk to you. I miss you so much my chest is on fire. If I were home, I'd Google, "can a 15-year-old get a heart attack" but there's no Google here, no Internet except at the library, which is in town almost 30 miles away. Grandma says they're exploring getting fiber optic Internet but it'll take a couple of years. In the meantime, we have to use the library Wi-Fi on Saturdays, if you can believe that. I'll FaceTime you then, so please answer.

And maybe, if it's not too bad here, you'll run away from Brooklyn and come live here with me? I could stand this place if you were here too.

In the meantime, I'm dying. Asphyxiating. Drowning.

### Evelyn

Day two of our new lives. I am bone tired. Marc and I worked on our bedroom, putting up the outside walls, cutting out holes for windows. David helped us for a while but then he had to repair the chicken coop, again. He offered to take us into town tomorrow to buy a couple of combination windows, which he warned us would cost two arms and a leg.

Resting on an Adirondack chair at the edge of the meadow, I'm trying to be Zen, all mindful breathing and calm. But my brain keeps slipping back to dinner last night, remembering how when we all get together around the dinner table, each of us turns into a cartoon parody of ourselves. Marc makes goofy jokes, which is marginally better than the silent treatment. Eloise hides one of my mother's gardening books on her lap and tries to read without anyone noticing. Rosie stares into space and I worry if her lungs feel tight or she's just off in the clouds again. She's a dreamy child, with imaginary friends she calls her ghost friends. Tillie scowls and refuses to make eye contact with anyone. Marc's parents make light conversation that ignores the herd of elephants crowding the room.

Lying on our futon mattress last night, attempting to find a comfortable position with the fold-lump under our backs, Marc and I whispered about what we've done, what I've done, and how will we live up here? Are there teaching jobs? Are there colleges near here? Whatever "near" means in this world. Or maybe we should both apply to teach at the high school. Or online, maybe, but no. There's no Wi-Fi. I can't imagine spending a long Maine winter all cooped up in this little house, with no jobs and no Internet.

This might have been a huge mistake, toxic wildfire air or not.

I swat mosquitoes, acknowledge my failure in the mindful breathing schtick, and go inside. I sneak my cell phone out of the suitcase and walk down the gravel road toward town, holding the phone high above my head in search of a signal. A caricature, right? No luck, so I walk back and use the house landline to call my sister in Brooklyn. I stretch the curly cord to its max to reach into the bathroom for privacy, like I did at home as a teenager, worried that the tension would rip the phone off the wall mount. I can barely talk though, just sob. When I emerge from the bathroom, Tillie is leaning against the wall opposite the door. Watching me.

"I thought landline calls were too expensive," she says. Not unkindly, for once.

"How about we can each make one call," I suggest. "To ease the transition."

## Sadie

Something is not right. Marc and Evelyn barely talk to each other. I can't help worrying that it's my fault, bringing them here. I know that's crazy; they're adults who make their own choices. But I worry.

Scientists say we carry trauma in our DNA and I believe that's true. My cells carry all the catastrophes of my people, going back forever. So Marc must inherit that genetic scar tissue too. Are we enriched by the chemicals of our histories circulating through our bodies, or hamstrung by them?

Worrying, I do the unforgivable mother/grandmother thing. When sweet Rosie and I are cuddled up on the porch swing after dinner, I ask her what's going on.

"It's my fault," she whispers. "I got sick and had to go to the hospital and Mom got really scared but Dad didn't want to come here. Now they're mad at each other."

"Of course it's not your fault, Rosie," I say, tucking her comment away to consider later. Rosie is an odd child, always has been, and her observations are often eerily spot-on.

David and I talk about it later in our bedroom, our voices hushed. Sound travels in nonlinear ways out here in the country, words riding small breezes out one window and in through another. Marc was never that interested in talking to us. Evelyn is usually more forthcoming, but now she's uncommunicative too.

I spend the day in the garden with my granddaughters. Last week I borrowed a tractor from our neighbor to triple the size of the garden, leaving the shovel and hand work to do together. When the twins get bored, I start them planting seeds. Tillie works hard for about two hours, then makes her hands bleed to get out of doing more. I remind her about wearing garden gloves, but she just tosses me that look, perfected by generations of teenage girls. Tillie reminds me of myself at that age and I ache for her, remembering the depths that roil under that hostile expression. My Lili perfected the look too, and it makes me miss my California daughter. I've been trying to convince her to move here next year—at least visit this summer.

By late afternoon, I can't ignore the ache in my back. I stow the garden tools and persuade the twins to help me make dinner. We chop onions and carrots and add them to the Dutch oven. Then I take two chickens from the fridge.

"They're not Grandpa's, are they?" Eloise asks, clasping her hands behind her back.

"No," I promise her. "Our chickens are for eggs. These come from the grocery store."

Her expression says she wants to believe me. She decides to help Rosie with the salad.

I don't have a clue what my son feels, working like a demon on winterizing the porch, making conversation impossible. And Evelyn seems so lost, the kids too, mourning their Brooklyn life. Was it the right thing to do? Moving here and gathering our family? I don't know.

But we will make this work. Because we must.

## Tillie

*J? Please pick up. I know you don't recognize this number—my grandma's landline—but please-please-please answer the phone.*

"Hello?"

"How'd you know it was me?"

"Area code for Maine. 207. I Googled it."

"Can you imagine living without Google? Or texting?"

"An adventure?"

"More like being banished to a prison island, like being dead."

"Come on, can't be that bad. It's pretty, isn't it?"

"I guess. But listen, my mom is going to apply for a teaching job. It was bad enough having her teach in the Brooklyn system. Here, it would be in my school."

"Ouch. Brutal."

"How's Silverbutt?"

"So fine. I love him."

"Does he miss me?"

"He hasn't said."

"Ha! So what's happening?"

"Nothing much."

"How's the air?"

"Still bad. The sky is yellow."

"Is Brooklyn under water yet?"

"No, but the subways are flooded. The whole F line."

"No shit! From rising seas?"

"Nah, from a wicked thunderstorm yesterday."

"Oh."

"It was bad. We had to take the bus."

"We who? Who are you hanging with? I've only been gone two days."

"You're still my bae. But I rode to school with Maggie and Sari. You want me to be alone all the time?"

*Yes*, I want to say. *Be miserable and lonely like I am.* Instead, I swallow hard and whisper, "Gotta go. It's dinner time. Love you."

I end the call, feeling worse than before. No one sees me leave the bathroom and slip out the back door. Black flies usually drive me crazy, but I barely notice them. I walk along the road, kicking up gravel so hard it stings my bare legs.

Evelyn

David drives Eloise and me to the building supply store. Eloise reads from the *Gazetteer* as we bounce along the rutted road.

"The Meetinghouse was built in 1800 and is an excellent example of a rural Gothic Revival church." Eloise pauses. "Sounds cool, Mom. Can we go there?"

"Sure, sweetie. After we get settled a bit."

It's hard to imagine being settled here. There's so much to do. New schools and jobs and dentists and doctors. Omigod, where's the closest hospital, in case Rosie has another bad attack? Probably hours away.

What have I done?

We buy the windows and Eloise chooses the paint for our new bedroom, a mauve shade that matches her dreamy personality more than Marc's or mine. My father-in-law already purchased most of the supplies to winterize the porch but didn't want to decide on color.

Driving back, I ask David about schools, where Marc and I should go to find out about teaching jobs. He seems surprised.

"You don't have to find work right away," he says. "We can feed you."

"Thank you, but we've got to register the girls. And we'll need work. Otherwise, we'll drive you and Sadie nuts."

Eloise interrupts. "Guess what? In October 2010, a man named Anders Olafson caught a rainbow trout in the Penobscot River weighing 8.42 pounds, breaking the record. Have you caught rainbow trout, Grandpa?"

"Sure, El. But never that big."

After we unload our purchases, I slip out the back door and take the path down to the pond. Despite everything hasty and distressing about this move, despite missing the bustle and familiarity of our old neighborhood, the earthy aroma of sprouting greens and the buzz of insects and the deep blue of the pond invite me to breathe and relax. I sit on a rock at the edge of the water, watching a family of ducks in the reeds. My mind wanders between Marc, Tillie, jobs, and telling myself not to waste this precious time alone worrying.

Ten minutes later, I hear rustling on the path and then my mother-in-law's voice.

"May I join you?" Sadie sits before I can answer. There goes my moment of peace and solitude.

"Are you and Marc okay?" she asks after a moment. "He doesn't talk to me."

"He's not talking to me much either." My voice cracks. I turn my head to watch a duck dive, tail feathers pointing to the sky. "He's really pissed that I insisted we leave the city immediately. Thinks I overreacted. Maybe I did. This move is really hard on the girls."

"Kids are pretty resilient." Sadie is silent for a few moments. "Do you ever regret your decision to have children? Because of climate change?"

Her question surprises me. I feel myself tighten up, getting defensive. "You had kids," I say. "Which is a very good thing for Marc. And me."

"Good for all of us," she says, her voice soft. "I have often wondered if David and I knew, when we were young, how bad things would get, if we would have chosen not to have kids."

"I always wanted children," I say. "Marc too. Even knowing what we knew. Maybe that's selfish of us, but would you prefer not to have your grandchildren in your life?"

The ducks look at us as if they're waiting for the answer.

"Of course not," Sadie says quickly. "And if I'm being honest with myself, I know I would have had kids anyway too. Family is more important to me than anything. I adore the girls."

"Tillie's hard to adore now, but she will be again, some day. If we all survive." I hesitate. I've always admired my mother-in-law, but our relationship is complicated. Sadie resents that I displaced her in Marc's affections, but isn't that the normal way of things?

"Maybe it *was* selfish," I admit." I had a pretty good idea that climate catastrophe was on our doorstep. "Not having kids because of what was coming would have felt like we were giving up, accepting that it's hopeless. I couldn't bear that."

"So," Sadie says slowly. "We keep abusing the earth and things keep getting worse."

"I know," I say. "Half my friends fly all over the world, clueless about their carbon footprint, and the other half are so judgy I can't stand it."

Sadie nods. "So we keep protesting and petitioning and writing letters to the editor and doing civil disobedience, decade after decade. And having kids and driving cars."

"You know what Tillie would say to that," I offer with a lopsided smile.

"Thirty years of blah, blah, blah," we quote in unison.

The ducks climb the grassy bank and waddle out of sight. I look across the pond into the deep northern forest and try not to be paralyzed by my fears. Partly about trying to make a life for ourselves in the middle of nowhere. But mostly about all of us on this beautiful burning, drowning, dying planet.

"Are we nuts?" I think about the disconnect between knowledge and despair. I miss Brooklyn but I want my daughters to have a chance at a full life. "We didn't bail after 9/11 and we didn't flee during Covid, but smoke poisons the air and we're outta there?"

Sadie touches my hand. I decide to take it as an apology of sorts and smile at her.

What I want to know is this: if an ordinary middle-class American family can be climate refugees, how can anyone on Earth be safe?

## Ellen Meeropol

### Sadie

Saturday morning is warm as we prepare the soil and plant seeds. The electrician installed the wiring yesterday, so Marc and Evelyn finish the drywall. In a day or two, they'll paint that soft mauve color. They seem a little less angry with each other, but I still have no idea what's going on. *Give them space,* I tell myself. Space is the only way to do this. But my conversation with Evelyn by the pond replays in my head, over and over. About children and hope.

This morning David went grocery shopping, Tillie and Rosie and I work in the garden, and Eloise reads to us from the *Gazetteer.* Got to expand that girl's reading material, which is the plan for the afternoon. Our first outing to the town library.

"Did you know that Benedict Arnold and his army were in Maine?" Eloise pushes her bangs out of her eyes as we gather our garden tools. "They had to carry their boats around the falls."

"I didn't know that," I say.

I wonder where the closest haircut place is. My hair is long and David goes to the barber in town. I bet the girls are used to a salon or something fancy.

"Why don't you girls take a break, go inside, and make lemonade?" I need a break. "It's almost lunch time."

The twins wash their hands at the pump, kick off their muddy clogs, and go into the kitchen. Tillie hangs back. When we're alone, she takes the terracotta terrier from her pocket and places it on a mound of earth.

"Did you leave this on my pillow, Grandma?"

"I thought you'd like it." I get up from the ground with difficulty and point at the porch swing.

"I do. Sort of." Tillie strokes the dog's stiff clay hair. "What's it about?"

I pause for a moment before answering. "It's a bisque piece. Half-fired, but never glazed. I don't know who made it, but my sister-in-law Liz, Emma's mom, found it in a potter's cottage on the island."

"How come I never met her?"

"She never lived on the island. Liz married my brother after he moved to Boston. Alan died young, and Liz was devastated. On a visit, Liz found the terrier and carried it in her breast pocket, like a talisman or mascot. She believed it brought her a second chance at life."

"What does that have to do with me?"

Suddenly, I need to speak honestly to my prickly granddaughter. From my heart. "Our people escaped ethnic violence in Europe. They built a life on the island and expected to be safe, but now that's in danger. You work hard all your life and you think you know how things will go. And then things happen, like losing people or they do things you don't understand, and the Earth is in big trouble with floods and fires and the pandemic, and I have this awful feeling that it's going to get a lot worse. None of the stuff you expected for your life is happening and you don't know how to make things right."

Tillie looks at me without a flicker of understanding in her eyes. Why am I talking like this to a 15-year-old? I force a laugh.

"I'm just blithering, sweetheart." I squeeze her hand. "I'm tired. Let's get that lemonade.

Tillie doesn't smile. "And you think I need him? The bisque doggie?"

"Do you?"

Tillie shrugs, picks up the terrier, and puts him into her breast pocket. I follow her into the house, hoping I've done the right thing.

Tillie

Dear Diary,

I give up. Give in. A week here and I'm writing in this stupid book. I'm pathetic.

I hate it here. If there was a way to run away home, I would do it in a minute. But according to the map, it's over twenty miles to the blacktop and ten more to the bus station in town. If I even had money for a ticket.

This afternoon we'll drive into town to the library. I wrote J that I'd FaceTime, but I don't know if they got the letter. I miss them so much, and my sweet kitty too. Maybe they've both already forgotten me.

I need to get books on different species of tomatoes and see what'll grow here. Who knew there were so many kinds of tomato plants? Grandma told me there's 4-H at the high school. Funny how something I wouldn't be caught dead doing at home might be barely acceptable in this place. Last night I asked her if there was a climate catastrophe group at the high school.

"Catastrophe?" she asked.

"Isn't it?"

"Yes," she admitted. "It is. For my island, for sure."

"Maybe like the kids who dress all in red and disrupt traffic? Not that there's any traffic here. I'd join any kind of climate group, probably."

She said maybe I'd have to start one.

On Monday, we'll go to the local school and register for next year. I can't imagine school without J.

"You'll make new friends here," Mom promises.

There's no one like J.

Speaking of people who need a friend, Mom seems lost. When she's not working her butt off, she stares off into nothing, like she's caught Rosie's spaciness. I get that she's upset. Dad's really pissed at her and I think she might worry that she did the wrong thing, insisting we leave right away. She should've listened to me.

My only friend here is this half-baked clay terrier. He goes everywhere with me, riding in my shirt pocket. He's used to that, from Liz, who had him before me. Our favorite place is the pond. Not the flat rocks at the end of the path where everyone goes. If you turn right and follow the reeds along the shore, there's a trickle of water from the hills and that leads to a mossy area. We sit there, the clay doggie and me, mostly in comfortable silence, but sometimes I talk to him. I tell him about wildfires and methane gas and rising sea levels, about my parents barely speaking to each other, about feeling like I'm drowning, like the island Grandma misses so much.

Sometimes, that drowning feeling is so strong that the world—my attic garrett or my mossy place—starts to melt, to be all fluid and wavy and wrong. Like I'm going to faint, or maybe there is another dimension trying to get through with something important to tell me. Something disastrous. When that happens, I hold the clay doggie next to my heart and close my eyes and the feeling passes.

Grandma says that the doggie is fragile because he's only half-fired. She suggested I repair his broken tail, glaze him, and fire him in the art room at the high school. But he doesn't feel fragile to me. He feels strong. Besides, cousin Liz left him like this and I agree.

I like him just the way he is.

# That Makes it an Island
## the island · 2018 · Laura

Sharing her island felt more intimate than sex. They'd been seeing each other for eight months, but Laura wasn't ready for Elijah to meet the island. Ever since he suggested moving in together a month earlier, she argued with herself about whether to invite him home to Maine.

The telephone call came on a sunny September morning as Laura was leaving for work. Her grandfather had a stroke.

"But Papa's so young," Laura had said.

"Sixty-three. It's medium bad," Grandma said from the hospital on the mainland. "He's out of immediate danger, coming home tomorrow. He'll need lots of care." Her voice got tough. "I've hired Emma to come over every day after school and help me, so don't quit your job or nothing." Then her voice softened. "Come home this weekend. And bring that young man."

Bringing Elijah home wasn't a simple thing. Laura hadn't yet mentioned to her grandparents that her boyfriend was Black. Not that it would matter, she hoped. But the palette of maritime Maine was steel-gray ocean, pine and fern green, granite and moss and waves and storm, and the subdued monochrome of pale-skinned folks.

The first time she met Elijah, he was singing. She rarely worked on the oncology floor and didn't know the staff. But Lucas had been her patient since he was a hamster-sized preemie and when he was diagnosed with leukemia, she continued doing his physical therapy. That day Laura's visit was mostly social, if you could call visiting a dying three-year-old social. The door to his isolation room was closed but she heard singing inside, a sad melody. She forced herself to don the paper gown, foot and head covers, mask and gloves, and open the door.

A nurse with tight black curls spilling from his isolation cap sat on the bed, rocking Lucas in his arms, bald head and IVs and tubes and monitor wires and all, and singing that sappy old song about a man walking in the rain clinging to his son's hand. The nurse looked at Laura, and his eyes smiled above the mask.

"I'm his P.T.," Laura said.

"He needs to sleep now. Come back later?"

"I have an opening at 3:00."

"Perfect. I'm Elijah, by the way."

Laura returned and did range-of-motion exercises with Lucas, gently stretching his elastic-band muscles. They did their usual routine—games and songs and chants—to pass the time, though Lucas dozed through most of it. Elijah returned after shift change and sat waiting on the parent bed-chair in the corner of his room until she finished.

"You have time for coffee?" His voice was tentative, but his brown eyes were certain.

The dregs of coffee cooled and skimmed over in thick white mugs as they sat on the patio of the café down the street from the hospital, early autumn leaves dancing at their feet. Coffee led to dinner and then every day together. Laura was shy and inexperienced, but Elijah was patient. Even though she was pushing thirty, the only guy she'd been with was an intern and she knew that was a mistake even before he started avoiding her in the hospital cafeteria. After the first time she and Elijah made love, lying in the tangled heat, pulses slowing, admiring the contrast in their skin tones, that's when she mentioned the island to him. To really know her, he had to know her home, her safe place, which huddled with its sister islands in the middle of Penobscot Bay.

After work on Friday, they caught the last boat from Rockland, and Grandma met them at the ferry terminal. As she drove to the white

## Sometimes an Island

clapboard house on Saperstein Neck, she warned Laura that Papa couldn't speak very well. She responded with a sharp look to Laura's reminder that Elijah was a nurse and they both worked in a hospital. Maybe being a male nurse would be harder for her grandparents to accept than his race?

When Laura leaned down to kiss Papa's cheek, half his face smiled, and he took her braid in his good hand. His hand, brown-spotted and calloused, held onto her braid as he shook Elijah's darker hand. Papa used to clasp her braid in two strong hands, fanning the wispy ends in the air as he made up stories about tiny sea elves that lived in abandoned barnacle homes in a land called Ticky-kicky-coin-coin. She rested her head on his chest, becoming that small girl leaning against Papa's arm, sitting close together on the barnacle-encrusted rocks at the cusp of forest and ocean. She sucked in a deep breath, the aroma of pinesap mixed with rotting sea life and his damp wool shirt.

"I'm home," she whispered, pushing back worries, "back in Ticky-kicky-coin-coin."

In the morning, she helped Papa eat. When he dozed, Grandma shooed Laura and Elijah out of the house. "Show your young man the island," Grandma said.

They walked in silence until Laura pointed to the two leaning birches on the right side of the dirt road. "That's the trailhead."

"Trailhead?"

"Where the trail begins." She ducked her head to lead him under a fir branch.

"Begins? We've been climbing hills for twenty minutes." Elijah followed her into instant deep forest. Thin blades of sunlight ignited sumac leaves along the dark path.

"Watch out!" She untangled the branch grabbing for Elijah's wire-rimmed glasses. "It's not far to Baby Sister Island. Not exactly an island, because you can walk to it at low tide. But the path is under water when the tide comes in. In Maine, that makes it an island."

"Why Baby Sister?"

"Our island and the two others nearby are called the Three Sisters. In the center of our island is the Basin, which fills and empties with the tides like a slow-beating heart. Baby Sister is snug inside the Basin—an island within an island. It's my family's favorite spot."

"Sweet," he said. "Even if it's only an island at high tide."

Laura smiled. "Papa named it, though it's not ours to name."

He took a deep breath. "What's that smell?"

"You don't have pines in Brooklyn?"

He laughed. "Gotcha!"

*Not funny,* Laura thought, then looked up at the oomph-thud of Elijah tripping, his stiff new hiking boots laughably clumsy on his long skinny legs.

"You okay?"

"Sure." He kicked at the exposed root snaking across the trail. "Tried to ambush me. Looks like a vein, doesn't it, waiting for an IV?"

"Can we forget work for the weekend?" They passed into a field of ferns, an extravagance of lace-patterned green that undulated like waves with the ocean breezes.

Elijah put his arm around her. "Come here, sweetheart. Let's fernicate."

She ignored him but even after all these months, she felt a catch of pleasure, like the night before when he grimaced at the sleeping arrangements. After kissing him goodnight and closing his bedroom door, Laura had gone back downstairs to sit with Grandma, who put down the seed catalogs and pad of numbers and patted the plaid sofa next to her.

"You like him?" Laura had asked, fingering her braid.

"Do you?"

"A lot. Maybe. Not sure." She rested her head on Grandma's shoulder. How could it be so bony and still so comforting?

Elijah's breathing came fast and raspy as they climbed.

"Over this last ridge and the Basin's just beyond." She slowed her pace to point out the lichen blooming in cauliflower shapes on the ballroom-sized ledges and the wisps of dusty green moss hanging like goatees from fir trees. And to let him catch his breath.

"When I was a kid," she said, "I thought these perfect circles of emerald moss were magic stepping stones. If I didn't step on every single one, Papa would die."

"Step on a crack, break your grandmother's back. That's what we said growing up in Brooklyn."

"Sometimes I can't believe you ever left." She tucked an escaping frizz of hair behind her ear. On the island, her hair soaked up moisture from the air and swelled into a tangled jungle.

He stroked her back. "But then I wouldn't have met you. So it was inevitable. Even the spiders are inevitable."

"That daddy longlegs last night really got to you, huh?" She crawled her fingers up his arm.

He brushed away her fingers. "I hate spiders."

"You don't shine in nature, do you?"

"You don't want me to, do you?"

The path across the ledge had widened enough for them to walk side by side, but they both looked straight ahead.

"What do you mean?"

"Ever since we stepped off that ferry, you've been pointing out what a city boy I am. But you knew that. So what gives? Is this some kind of test?"

Laura turned away, toward the Basin, searching through dense leaves for a glimpse of soft blue. Was he right? Was she looking for proof that he didn't belong here? Grandma had urged her to bring him home in case Papa died, so they could at least meet. Why was Laura so reluctant? Was it a betrayal of her island to love a city boy?

Laura had accompanied Elijah to his parents' Brooklyn brownstone last Thanksgiving. Sitting in their bookshelf-lined living room, she had pointed at the portrait over the mantel.

"Benjamin Elijah Mays," he told her.

"A relative?"

He shook his head. "A civil rights leader and educator. He was president of Morehouse College when my dad attended. He mentored Reverend King. I'm named after him. Too bad they didn't choose Benjamin."

"I've never heard of him," Laura admitted.

On that visit, the differences between their families swelled and widened and flooded until it felt like an ocean and Laura couldn't remember how to swim. When Elijah asked again last month to visit her family, she couldn't answer. Papa's stroke decided for her, but she still couldn't answer his question. Was this a test?

"Look." She touched his shoulder and pointed at the tease of blue between the shifting leaves.

"The Basin?"

"Uh-huh." She pointed again. "And there's the path to Baby Sister. The tide is low, so the trail's dry." They would have to hurry to get back before the tide came in.

Sliding down the pebbly slope, they followed the narrow path bordered by mudflats and a small beach of silt-covered mussel shells. A heron stood poised in the shallow water, watching from her shadowed fishing spot. Elijah's nostrils flared at the smell of decaying shellfish, but he didn't mention it.

They picked their way over jumbled granite rocks to the point end of the small island and climbed the flat bed-sized boulder with its high tide ring of barnacles. The rock jutted into the gray-green water, iced with the smashed remains of a seagull feast.

"Let's eat." She put down the backpack and sat.

"Here? With all this bird crap?" He surveyed the stone, looking for the least foul area. He ducked as a herring gull swooped close and squawked his complaint. "No wonder he's dive-bombing us. We're sitting in his bathroom."

"This is one of the most beautiful views on the island." Pulling a faded Indian print bedspread from the backpack, from her childhood bedroom before Grandma turned it into her sewing room, she spread it on the rock, then opened a bag of cut-up vegetables.

"Harbor seal." She pointed with a carrot stick.

"Where?"

She leaned close. "See the brown head, just to the left of those pointy rocks? His nose jutting into the air? Oops, he dived, but keep watching. He'll be back. Keep these handy." She slipped the cracked leather binoculars strap around his neck and handed him a sandwich. They chewed in silence, watching the slow ripples of water reflect the oblique sunlight.

"Laura..."

"Uhm?"

"I know your grandparents raised you. But you've never told me what happened to your parents."

She wasn't exactly ashamed of her mother. Well, maybe a little, when she compared her sparse and oddly shaped gathering of kinfolk to Elijah's orderly and well-leafed family tree. Growing up, she didn't have to explain anything. Island life could be harsh and other kids came from mangled families too. Grandma said there was a girl in school with Mom whose father was in prison. Ruby hadn't known her well, but Grandma said she was kin to them. Island kids called that girl the jailbird's daughter, but they left her alone.

They left Laura alone too, and that was okay. She went home after school to do her chores and hang out with Papa. She helped him on the farm and they took long walks together, making up stories about sea elves and magical barnacle-boats. The year she was twelve, Papa's tractor hit a rock and he fell off and broke his leg in two places. After the cast came off, the physical therapist came out from the mainland twice a week on the ferry. She was so gentle with him, and Laura knew that was the work she wanted to do.

"Not sure where to start," Laura said. "My family has been islanders for generations."

She grew up hearing all the stories, about how her great-great-grandfather, his two best friends, and a ten-year-old girl escaped the pogroms in their shtetl and came to America, to their island. The men got jobs as stone workers but then concrete was invented and it was so much cheaper than shipping huge carved granite blocks to big cities for their post offices and churches and libraries. The quarries couldn't compete.

"When the quarries closed, my great-grandfather started a farm. Old Granite Farm, he called it. People laughed because the soil here is more stone than earth. His sons hated the work, except Papa." Laura wanted him to understand how special her grandfather was.

"He loved the land and growing things. My mother was born when he and Grandma were young, just married. Grandma says Ruby, my mom, was always stormy, determined from a young age to leave the island and live in a big city. She got pregnant when she was a teenager and refused to name the father. She left when I was a baby."

Laura's voice felt rusty. She had been told the story for years but had never said the words out loud. How her mother got up early that morning, walked into town, and caught the ferry. How Grandma swore that she knew the second she opened her eyes that morning that her daughter was gone, even before she found Laura sleeping on the sofa, and then found Mom's favorite sweatshirt and Laura's pink bunny suit spread out on seagull rock, Mom's favorite place to sit and daydream, staring off toward the mainland.

"Grandma says we were lucky she left the bunny suit there overnight, all crusty with seagull shit, instead of me. No one has heard from my mother since."

"You must miss her."

"I don't remember much about her."

An osprey circled in the cloud-free sky. Laura pictured Elijah's parents, deep in animated conversation in their living room crowded with artsy black and white photos, bookshelves climbing all the way to the ceiling.

"My grandparents raised me. They were in their early thirties when I was born, and they always insisted I call them Mary and Caleb or Grandma and Papa, so that if my mother came back for me, everything would be clear."

"But she didn't?"

Laura shook her head. Aspen leaves rustled in the wind like brittle paper.

She was glad he didn't say anything. Grateful that instead he slipped his hand under her sweatshirt and found her nipple and soon she didn't have to talk either. His mouth erased the familiar but impossible image behind her eyes, of herself sitting with her mom and Papa on Seagull Rock. How was it possible for a baby to remember, she had always wondered, before the edges of the memory fizzed and faded?

Laura stretched out on the warm rock, using the pack as a pillow. Her skin felt liquid and her bones relaxed. She kissed him again, grateful that she didn't have to think or remember. She didn't want to tell him the rest of the story, the part she hadn't known until the night before, and still didn't quite believe. Had that really happened, sitting with Grandma and her seed catalogs on the plaid sofa late last night, with the backdrop of Papa's leaden breathing in the next room?

"Maybe I'm just scared," Laura had whispered. "To trust him."

"Maybe you can't trust anyone. Because of your mom." Grandma tucked an escaping curl behind Laura's ear.

"I trust you guys," Laura said, smiling at Grandma.

Grandma didn't smile back. "No. Listen." She looked straight ahead at the empty dark square of the living room window. "Caleb thinks he's dying. He wants you to know."

"Know what?"

"You weren't a baby when your mother left," Grandma said. "You had just turned three. Your mom was still living with us, miserable and misbehaving something awful. She entertained her men on Seagull Rock, while toddler-you played with the shells on the shore nearby. Papa found her there late one evening and brought you back to the house. That night, he put down his foot. In the morning, your mom was gone."

This version immediately felt true, and the truth excavated her chest. It was so much worse for her mother to leave her at almost three. At three she would be a real person, with speech, a personality. She thought about Lucas, his delicious quirks and verbal silliness.

How could her mother leave her at three?

"What about the story about my pink bunny suit on the rock? About me being just a baby?"

"I made that up," Grandma had said.

When Laura opened her eyes, dusk smudged the line between shore and sky, like a thumb on a charcoal drawing. Next to her, Elijah propped himself on one elbow, rubbing his eyes with the other hand. The sea breeze had blown in wispy thickets of fog, with a damp autumn chill on its breath.

"High tide?" he asked. Soft waves slapped their rock.

"Shit. I'm sorry. We're stuck here until the tide goes out."

"How long?"

"Five, six hours. And then we walk back in the dark." Laura pulled two windbreakers from the backpack and tested the small flashlight. They put on the jackets and scooted closer together on the damp rock surface.

"Sorry," she said again. "I should have paid attention." No, that wasn't entirely honest. She could have roused herself to get back in time. She knew the tide tables like her body's monthly rhythm.

"Are you worried?" he asked.

"Not really. We'll be fine. We have crackers and veggies and cheese and water." She tried to smile at him. Would they be fine?

"Will your grandma worry?"

"Not too much. I hope." Grandma knew where they were

headed. Elijah was probably the only one who was worried. Was this another test?

"We'll keep each other warm." He put his arms around her and started singing softly.

Daylight was almost gone, just a streak of salmon resting for a moment on the fog-blurred lilac water. Laura shifted her position on the crusty rock and listened to Elijah sing about pastures of plenty. She rubbed her forehead on his scratchy cheek and tried to imagine his brownstone parents sitting in her grandparents' living room watching the herons hunt at dusk. Maybe his parents would visit for Thanksgiving. They'd stop at Bean on the way up and buy hiking boots. They would appreciate feasting on a local turkey rather than a frozen supermarket bird. Maybe Grandma would tell them family stories about farming granite and her wild daughter who left and how Laura decided to become a physical therapist.

Those things might happen. In the dark night, she might find the words to tell him the rest of the Ruby story, the part that had been long hidden from her. As he cradled her, making a soft nest, a rocky refuge on Baby Sister Island, she melted her knobby backbone into the curve of his chest, cushioned by his calm. This night together on the rock might tell her what she needed to know. Maybe they could find a sheltered path between high and low tides, between island and brownstone, between history and the new stories to come. Between sometimes an island and sometimes not.

# Gridlock
the co-op · 2019 · Miriam

My sister Ruth showed up on day four of the blackout, the day we began to suspect this wasn't an ordinary grid failure. There had been no blizzard, no major wind event. It wasn't even that cold, though the early November air already held the crisp-edged fragility of the coming western Massachusetts winter. The utility company issued no reassuring texts about the prompt restoration of power and there were no earnest promises from the mayor.

At our co-op meeting two nights before, we discussed how to handle people seeking shelter in the converted factory building where Samuel and I lived with twenty other people, including our son Ben and his wife Sarah. Ben was obsessed with climate disaster, so we were off-the-grid and mostly self-sustaining. He'd been collecting cots and blankets and stockpiling food for something just like this—whatever it was. At the meeting we decided to keep the outside doors locked, take turns keeping watch, and set up a shelter in the community wing. People in town knew we had heat and electricity and we expected neighbors to show up—about three dozen people so far—but we never anticipated Ruth. My sister and I hadn't seen each other in over fifty years.

When Ruth arrived, I was on lookout duty. From an armchair atced the front window, I watched a road-filthy electric car with New York plates pull into the parking lot, the asphalt surface glittery in the oblique afternoon light. With the grid down, I wondered how they expected to charge the battery and get back home. I recognized Ruth the moment she climbed out of the driver's side. Her red curls had gone rusty gray, but the fire still blazed.

I punched the "All" button on the intercom system. "We got company," I announced. "Samuel, Ben, it's Ruth."

Ruth strode across the parking lot with the gait of a top-of-the-food-chain lioness, only minimally slowed by age or infirmity. She was three years older than me, making her seventy-seven, but despite a slight limp she exuded the vitality of a much younger woman. I tried to read her expression as she studied our building's eclectic mix of antiquated and innovative: stained factory brick with heavy plastic secured over the old multi-pane windows and the soccer-field sized roof divided between a mammoth photovoltaic array and a passive solar greenhouse. Not beautiful, but one of the few places in town with power. I unlocked the double metal doors and faced her. The ten feet of empty air between us froze my heart and sizzled with energy.

Time folded back on itself and for a moment it was 1968. I was a young mother on a city street heavy with tear gas, convinced by my older sister to join her in throwing rocks at police beating anti-war protestors. I blinked my eyes to banish the memory and swallowed the familiar emotions—confusion and fury, guilt and longing.

Ruth's expression displayed no burden of memory. "Miriam!" Her voice boomed and she enveloped me in a monster hug.

I tried to pull away. "How'd you know where we live?"

She didn't let go. "That piece from the *Times* last year."

Our co-op had argued about that article, one of those alternative lifestyle features with the tone so nuanced you couldn't decide whether they were admiring or ridiculing our lives. The younger members were proud of it, but Samuel and I were leery of the publicity. We knew it might lead to some people seeking us out. We never expected Ruth.

Ruth grinned. "Who'd have thunk that *you'd* be the one to be living in a commune."

I studied her face, trying to decide if she was insulting me. It was hard to know with Ruth; she was as magnetic as she was destructive. I led her around the leftover Halloween decorations toward the mismatched grouping of easy chairs and couches ringing

*Sometimes an Island*

the wood stove in our co-op living room, once the massive lobby of a brush factory. Alone with Ruth in that huge space, I wished Samuel would show up. I hoped Ben would hear the intercom in the basement where he was working on our photovoltaic storage system. But Ben and Sarah knew the story of Ruth and me. I wouldn't blame them for choosing any other task over my meshugganah sister.

"Where's Samuel?" Ruth asked.

"He'll be down in a moment. What about Cornell?"

"In the car. Should I invite him in?"

"Sure. It's cold out there."

"Thanks." Ruth opened her mouth and then stopped. She probably wanted to ask if they could stay. I wondered how my famous sister liked having the power in the *other* sister's hands for a change and if I was petty to feel satisfaction at the reversal.

Ruth returned with Cornell, who dumped their duffle bags and backpacks on the floor. Did she think they could just move in with us? Cornell hadn't changed that much, although his Afro and wiry beard had turned snow white. It was easy to welcome him; when we were young, Cornell had always managed to smooth out some of Ruth's sharp edges. I had no idea what to say to either of them.

My husband had good timing. He strode into the room and opened his arms to Ruth and Cornell. "Welcome to our home," he said.

I was enormously proud of Samuel at that moment, of his generosity. Samuel had always been fiercely protective of my feelings and hugely critical of Ruth. "That woman is toxic," he liked to say. Coming from a pediatrician who dealt with the havoc caused by microbial toxins on a regular basis, that label meant something and it had stuck. Toxic Ruth.

"So what's up with this blackout?" she asked.

Samuel shook his head. "No idea. But I'm pretty worried. Something feels very wrong."

Ruth laughed. "You always specialized in worry. I'm sure the power will be back soon."

The kettle whistled. As our guests busied themselves with hot drinks, Ben and Sarah appeared in the doorway.

Ben and Sarah were fiftyish, but they felt way out of their league when Ruth was involved. We rarely talked about that part of the family. Rarely like never. Ben brought in firewood and filled the stove. Sarah lit the kerosene lanterns against the gathering dusk.

Cornell waved his arm around the cavernous room. "What *is* this place?"

Ben leaned forward, resting his elbows on his knees. "It's off-the-grid communal living. We collect solar energy and store it, so we're self-sufficient. With two wells, wood stoves, rooftop gardens, greenhouses, and chickens, we grow or raise most of our food. This is our co-op living room."

"Who lives here?" Ruth asked.

"Seven families have apartments upstairs," Sarah said.

"But since the power went out," Samuel added, "about thirty-five neighbors are here."

"Where are they all?" Cornell asked.

Sarah pointed to the hallway. "Down that corridor is the public half of the building: two event rooms, bathrooms, storage space, and a restaurant-sized kitchen. We've got plenty of cots and blankets and water."

"How can you put up all those people?" Ruth asked.

"They're our neighbors," Ben said. "They brought bedding and air mattresses and food. They've organized meals and clean-up and childcare."

"Aren't there shelters in town?" Cornell asked.

Ben nodded. "One at the high school and one at City Hall. But they just have a couple of generators. Since the blackout is so widespread, the Red Cross is stretched awfully thin."

"What about us," Ruth asked. "Can you put us up?"

"For a night or two, sure," I said. "Beyond that, the group will decide."

After coffee and tea and clean-up, I showed Ruth and Cornell to the empty apartment on the second floor, kept minimally furnished for visiting family and holiday guests.

Ruth stood at the huge factory windows, looking towards the last smudge of pink outlining the western hills. "This is an amazing view. And this apartment is perfect for us."

"Decisions about adding new folks," I reminded her, "are made at a co-op meeting."

"But we're here already," Ruth argued. "And we really need a place to stay."

## Sometimes an Island

"There's an assisted living facility down the road about to run out of gas for their generator. Those people are old and they need a place to stay too."

Ruth chuckled. "Trying to save the whole world, little sister?"

"Someone has to do it. Once that would have been you."

"Touché," Ruth said.

"Why are you here? There must be a shelter closer to home."

"Because you're family," Ruth said. Cornell touched her arm, to shut her up maybe, and I wondered if he could still get away with that. No one else had ever been able to.

"We make our decisions together here. Surely *you* can understand that."

Sharp words, but I wondered why she and Cornell drove three hours to our home. Then the guest alarm sounded, and Albie's voice on the intercom sounded more frantic than usual.

"Incoming," he shouted. "Need backup."

"Got to go," I told Ruth and Cornell. "Dinner at 6:00."

Albie was a vet from the first Iraq war and easily spooked. He was a whiz with anything mechanical and with no Internet, his ham radio hobby was invaluable. His wife was Sarah's best friend, and their Myesha was the closest I'd ever get to a granddaughter. I hurried downstairs.

Albie's incoming was a mother and three kids pulling a red wagon piled with boxes of cereal and raisins, cans of soup and soda. The youngest, about six, hugged a stuffed unicorn. Myesha arrived first. She knew the oldest girl and soon they were whispering. Sarah and I exchanged glances and backed out of the crowded room. Myesha would bring her friend's family down the hall to the public area and find them cots and blankets.

Sarah and I sat in our favorite chairs by the wood stove.

"Do you want Ruth to stay?" Sarah asked.

"I don't know."

"After all, she's your sister."

"Yes." I squeezed my eyes closed. "She is my sister."

Normally we didn't all eat together every night, but we were trying to conserve energy and food. We passed large bowls of rice and beans and veggies down the long table.

I sat between Ben and Samuel, as far away from my sister as I could manage. I wasn't hungry, hadn't really been hungry since the grid went down. What would happen if people could never again turn on the lights or listen to music or answer an email? Luckily, my co-op chairperson role kept me so busy I didn't have time to seriously consider the possibility that the grid failure was permanent. That just couldn't happen, could it?

"I have a question," Ruth said above the dinnertime chatter. "What happens when the food runs out? Or when more people want to move in than you have room for? Or if...?"

I knew what she was asking. It's what we all worried about, but no one wanted to say out loud: what happens if the power doesn't return? What if this was the way life would be from now on?

"Right, because a lot of people must know you've got electricity and heat," Cornell added. "What if people try to force their way in?"

Ben stood up. "Those are great questions and they're on the agenda for tonight's meeting. I'm on the clean-up crew, so I'm going to get started." At his words, everyone pitched in. By a few minutes after seven, the dishes were done and we were gathered around the stove, without our guests.

I started the meeting by asking Ben to report on our physical plant and energy supplies. When he stood up to speak, the concrete in my chest softened a little. Ever since he was a toddler, my son reminded me of a Dr. Seuss drawing, with a major cowlick and a goofy grin. The Ben character would have a hedgehog head on a giraffe's body. He would spout rhymes, updating the *Lorax* to our current situation, making us laugh and not worry so much. But the real-life Ben had been acting odd recently, even before the blackout, and it triggered my worry genes like mad.

"Two things I want to tell you," he said. I loved how everyone listened to him. I hoped he would be able to pull us together, to remind us why we created this place. "The good news is that our food and energy supplies are terrific. The batteries are over 90% full, the solar water pumps are fine, and the photovoltaic array is working perfectly. Our permaculture garden is still giving us veggies, even in November. A lot of the credit for that goes to Jeremy."

Jeremy and his girlfriend Zoe were the newest co-op members. Jeremy originally came to us for an independent study as part of his grad school program and we loved him and Zoe, who was finishing up nursing school.

But really, my son was the reason we were so well prepared. I was proud of him, even if I still didn't quite understand his insistence on being off-the-grid, which started after he went to California last year for a climate change conference. He stayed a couple of extra days and came home freaked out about climate denial. He talked about infrastructure collapse until my eyes glazed over, and his whispered conversations with Jeremy increased.

Ben's mouth turned down at the corners. "There's some not-so-good news too. Albie has been monitoring shortwave radio transmissions. A huge chunk of the country is dark, from Virginia to Maine and west almost to Chicago. Washington is crippled, and the financial centers in Manhattan. There seems to be an interim federal government somewhere in Colorado, and there are rumors of a stock exchange operating out of Los Angeles."

His voice got quiet, and he looked around the circle.

"So what are you saying?" I prompted, knowing from his expression that there was more.

In the silence we could hear the wind blow sleety snow against the big factory windows. "I'm saying that this is worse than we originally thought." He glanced at Albie. "And it might not have been an accident."

His announcement was met with silence.

"You mean someone crashed the grid on purpose?" Sarah asked. "Why?"

"I'm not saying they *did*," Ben said. "Just that it's possible." He sat down abruptly.

"Next item on the agenda is Ruth and Cornell," I said. "Should we invite them to stay?"

There wasn't much discussion. Usually, we follow a slow process of getting to know prospective members of the community, over weeks and months of discussions and shared meals and work. But this wasn't usual.

As we talked, Ben looked down, as if he had some kind of secret knowledge and couldn't trust his features to keep it hidden. How did my son even have an opinion about why the blackout happened and how long it would last? I studied his face. His new round granny-glasses made him look even more like a Dr. Seuss character. A very troubled one.

Albie raised his hand. "What kind of skills do these New Yorkers have?"

Sarah consulted her clipboard. "Ruth is a political organizer. And taught GED classes."

"Maybe she could help Miriam with the school," someone called out.

*Maybe not,* I thought.

"You should know," Samuel announced, "that Ruth taught GED classes in prison."

That was a conversation-stopper. Everyone stared at me and my face flamed. "It's a long story, but I can promise you she doesn't pose any threat."

"Debatable," Samuel muttered, barely audible. I suppressed a smile, oddly glad that Samuel was back to his fierce protector role.

"Cornell is an attorney," Sarah said. "Both he and Ruth say they're willing to do whatever we need. They know that we're each volunteering five hours a day during this crisis."

"Maybe the lawyer could have permanent bathroom duty," someone suggested. We all laughed.

The discussion went around for a while, but consensus was reached without too much difficulty: Ruth and Cornell could stay for the duration of the blackout. We decided to invite the assisted living folks to the public wing, along with their caretakers.

After the meeting, I puttered around the kitchen, rinsing cups and wiping down the counters. Sarah stood behind me, hugging me.

"What's up?" I asked.

"Don't know," she said. "But I'm worried that Ben might have expected the blackout."

Her words made sense. Several months ago, Ben started insisting we stock up on beans and grains, can more veggies and fruits, stockpile extras of the things we can't live without. He told us to double up on prescription drugs and toilet paper, and replace devices that require electricity with ones that don't, like grinding our coffee beans by hand.

I tried to unwrap Sarah's arms so I could see her face, but she resisted and spoke to the back of my head. "Ever since that conference, he's been doing odd things. Like giving up his contact lenses for glasses."

"And he gave you that vintage typewriter for your birthday, with a lifetime supply of ribbons, and ordered me a case of batteries for my hearing aids. He even suggested to Zoe that she order reusable metal catheters for her spina bifida, instead of the usual plastic ones. Looking back, it's almost as if he knew this was coming." I swiveled to face Sarah. "Have you asked him what's going on?"

"Last night. He evaded the question, changed the subject."

"Ask again. He adores you."

"I used to think Ben and I shared everything." Sarah buried her sad face in my hair. "You'd think I would know, from what happened to you and Ruth, that people who are close can be horribly divided, can lose each other."

I was glad she couldn't see my expression when she said that. No matter how I tried to understand what happened with Ruth and me, the kernel—the truth—eluded me. We had been the closest of sisters, at home and summer camp and college. It was always Ruth and Miriam, and then it was Ruth and Miriam and Cornell and Samuel.

Together, we were going to change the world. But that summer day in 1968, the world changed us. Ruth and I were at a huge anti-war demonstration when the cops started beating up protestors. A few people began throwing rocks to stop the beatings and Ruth joined them. I didn't want to, but I couldn't bear for Ruth to think I was less committed than she was to the anti-war struggle. So I threw a rock too. A cop was hurt, and we were arrested.

Ruth and I disagreed about what to do. Ben was a baby and I couldn't stand the thought of being separated from him, so I accepted a plea bargain. That meant I had to testify in court, to tell what happened, what we did. I told the truth, but Ruth was furious with me. She went underground, then was caught and went to prison, becoming a heroine in lefty circles. She has never forgiven me. I'm not sure I've forgiven myself.

Sarah hugged me again. "I know you tried to reconcile."

"And failed. And now she shows up here."

On day six of the blackout, the weather turned colder. The previous few years had been warmer than average, and we were no longer used to single-digit temperatures. We told ourselves that's why the governor called a state of emergency. They called it *shelter in place*, but everyone knew what curfews meant. Without television or radio stations broadcasting, without access to the Internet, getting information was challenging. Police cars with roof-mounted loudspeakers drove up and down the streets announcing that citizens were to stay inside their homes or community shelters, except for a daily window from noon to 4:00 pm. Starting immediately. They didn't say why, but we assumed desperate people were looting for food and firewood.

Over lunch that day we had an impromptu meeting about this new development. Sarah, who runs the local food pantry, suggested we open our doors to the community for a hot lunch as long as we had enough rice and beans to share. How would we let people know?

Myesha jumped up. "We can do that. The teen brigade will write leaflets and distribute them all over town. We'll use our bikes."

I was too tired to budge. Ruth stood close to Sarah in the kitchen, laughing.

I felt Samuel's hand on my shoulder.

"Even pushing eighty, she has this sizzle of energy, doesn't she?" I whispered.

Ben and Albie interrupted us. The dark expressions on their faces silenced the room.

"Listen up," Ben said. "Important announcement."

"News from the shortwave radio." Albie said. "Six other states declared martial law today."

Over the next twenty-four hours, we settled two dozen elderly people into a curtained-off corner of the smaller event room, along with caregivers, wheelchairs, walkers, and a blue rolling cabinet of medications and supplies. More people than I could count—more than I wanted to know—showed up for the first free hot lunch. Some of them brought sleeping bags and simply didn't leave. It wasn't until late that night that I actually saw one of Myesha's leaflets. My surrogate granddaughter had added an unauthorized sentence at the bottom: *If you're desperate, bring your food and wood and sleeping bags or blankets. You won't be turned away.*

The day's pleasant surprise was Cornell. He found me warming my feet by the stove late Thursday evening and sat down.

"You look beat," he said. "I want to help."

"You worked in the greenhouse today, didn't you?"

"Sure, and I'm happy to do that, but I'd like to do more. You seem overwhelmed."

## Sometimes an Island

I closed my eyes. Cornell was right. I couldn't ever remember feeling so tired and stressed. I'd been half-dozing over my clipboard, trying to figure out the next day's work assignments. Trying to stretch our resources and energy. Trying not to think about how Ben seemed to know about this blackout mess before it happened.

Cornell touched my shoulder and my eyes jerked open.

"I'm a decent manager," he said. "With more people coming, it's going to get more complicated. I can make job lists, collect reports from people." He grinned and pointed at my clipboard. "I can help with the assignments. I can even type."

I was surprised. My primary memory of Cornell was of arrogance.

"We just happen to have a typewriter," I said. "Maybe we could work together first thing in the morning and then meet again after you're done in the garden." I paused. "You don't get off greenhouse duty for this, you know."

"Wouldn't think of it," Cornell said. "Turns out I like digging in the dirt."

The next morning, Friday, day seven of the blackout, we ate oatmeal with reconstituted powdered milk, and Albie announced that his shortwave radio buddies predicted unseasonably cold weather heading our way. He read a short statement from Ben announcing that a freeze would severely tax our stored energy. The first priority was to provide minimal heat to the building, enough to keep the pipes—and us—from freezing.

Cornell and I exchanged looks and poured ourselves more coffee. I asked Albie where Ben was.

"He and Jeremy are working on some problem with the battery settings."

"When you see him," I said, "tell him to come find me."

Cornell and I revised the work charts, assigning extra people to prepare the greenhouses for frigid weather. Then Cornell went to put up the charts and I headed to the shelter wing to the makeshift school, where thirty children ranging from two to sixteen were writing stories on yellow pads and building rocket ships with cartons and duct tape. Ruth and Zoe were helping the oldest kids with reading and I had promised a painting class. I was too busy to think about what Ben knew and how.

Late that evening, Sarah knocked on our apartment door. She

was wrapped in a down comforter and her face was grim. Ben towered behind her, looking as serious as a Seuss character could manage. Samuel and I were already in our pajamas. The four of us settled in the circle of comfortable chairs, draped in bathrobes and comforters against the chill. Two thick beeswax candles lit the space.

Sarah sat as far from Ben as she could in the small space. "Tell them what you told me."

Ben looked at his hands, clasped in his lap. "I'm sorry I couldn't share this before."

"Tell us now," I said.

"Things are so much worse than I thought. More complicated. Global warming and species extinction and icecap loss and drought and famine." He stopped to clear his throat, as if the whole beautiful dying Earth was caught there.

"At the California climate conference Jeremy and I went to last year, some people tried to convince us that carbon caps and solar panels could save us, but the numbers didn't add up." He swiped at his eyes. "It became clear that we've got to do so much more than light bulbs and carbon caps. But I didn't know how to make those changes." His words trailed off.

"And then," I prompted him.

"Then I met some people with a plan. Anarchists but incredibly well-organized. After the 2008 collapse they realized that our buy-more, throw-away economic system is causing the climate problems. They reorganized their town so that everyone works half-time. Most people are employed and with their other time they make stuff. Stuff they would have bought before. Like clothes and pottery and food and music. It's very cool."

"What difference does one town make?"

He leaned closer. "These folks are part of a network of activists, mostly in California and the Pacific Northwest. They've got technological expertise, engineering and hydrology especially. A bunch of towns are now using their model. Over time, it could make a big difference. And working fewer hours, people have more time for family and friends. They're happier." His eyes glistened. I couldn't tell if it was tears or excitement.

"Who are these anarchists?" Samuel asked.

He shook his head. "I can't tell you that. I promised. But I spent a few days with them after the conference. I read their material, their manifesto, and... I joined them."

"What does this secret group have to do with what's going on?" Sarah's voice was controlled, but furious.

"I can't tell you that either," he whispered. "Not yet."

"Then you and I are in big trouble." Sarah stood up and pulled the comforter closer around her shoulders. It was thick and soft, a gift from Samuel and me last Chanukah. "I thought you and I were completely honest with each other, Ben. That we didn't keep secrets."

"Where are you going?" he asked.

"I'll sleep downstairs," Sarah said. She wrapped our holiday present around her angry and lonesome self.

When I arrived downstairs the next morning to make coffee, Sarah was sleeping on the plaid sofa, cocooned in her comforter. By the time the coffee was brewed, her eyes were open.

I brought two mugs to the sofa. She moved her feet to give me room, then sat up and accepted her mug.

"You okay?"

"Ruth couldn't sleep last night either. She came downstairs and we talked. I loved hearing her version of events."

"Like what?"

"Everything. Growing up. All the stuff you guys did, helping women get abortions and anti-war marches."

I looked at her sharply, almost spilling my coffee.

"Yes," Sarah said. "We talked about *that* day."

I could imagine.

"How are *you* doing, having Ruth here?" Sarah asked. "It must be so weird."

"Totally. We once knew each other inside out. Now I haven't a clue what she's thinking."

"Have you talked?"

I shrugged. "She lectured me about the big women's march."

"I can't see Ruth in a pink pussy hat!"

I didn't laugh. "And she won't stop asking me about grandchildren."

"What do you tell her?"

"That you and Ben think there are already enough people in the world." I shook my head. "I *hate* it when Ruth feels sorry for me."

"Do you know why she's here? Really, I mean?"

"No clue."

"Have you talked about the past?" Sarah let her voice slide away into the land of unspoken places.

I shook my head.

"How can you live like that?"

"Lots of practice."

Ten minutes later, Samuel and I dawdled over our coffee, already wearing our layers of long johns and thermal shirts and wool socks. Cornell and Ruth pawed through a mountain of long underwear and fleece pants and lined sweatshirts and double thick wool socks piled on the green plaid sofa. The deep freeze was as bad as predicted.

"Dibs on the red one." Ruth held up a union suit, fanny flap open like a lopsided grin.

"Big surprise," Samuel muttered.

Ben whistled and the room quieted. "Two things you should all know before we get started on the day's work. The temperature and wind chill are even worse than predicted so stay inside. After nine days, the town shelters are running dangerously low on supplies. Also, Albie has been monitoring the shortwave radio conversations and it sounds like the Commonwealth is starting to take over privately owned resources, claiming the emergency."

"Damn them," Albie said. "We're already feeding and housing half the town."

"Even so, the emergency probably gives them the legal right," Ben said.

As the meeting broke up, Ruth touched my shoulder. "Can we talk?"

We settled on two mismatched easy chairs in the small alcove off the living room, facing each other. Ruth looked tired.

"I'm sorry if I said anything to Sarah last night, anything I shouldn't have."

"Ruth apologizing? Alert the media!"

"Have I thanked you enough?" Ruth said. "For taking us in? I don't know what we would have done if you guys sent us away."

"You're welcome," I said after a long pause. "I'm glad you're here. Mostly."

Ruth ignored the last word. "I love your community, how you all work together. It reminds me of us, our old collective and the women's group and our potluck dinners and meetings."

"Before," I said.

"Before."

"I wish you had visited sooner," I said. "When things were normal."

"What do you miss most from that normal life?"

"Having time to paint," I said. "What about you?"

Ruth laughed. "Now you'll see how shallow I've become. I miss that little thingie that froths the milk for my coffee. You press a button and you've got a latté."

*Samuel would love that,* I thought. *If life goes back to normal, I'll find that gadget and bring him coffee with frothed milk in bed every morning.*

"Why now?" I asked.

Ruth shrugged. "We're old. I'm tired."

"I have something I want to give you," I said. "I've been writing to you for years, ever since you wrote me that first horrible letter after the trial. I didn't mail any of them. At first I didn't know where to find you, and then it was just too late."

"I kept a journal," Ruth said. "I brought it with me."

We were interrupted by Albie. "We need you now, Miriam. Big problem."

I followed him to the dining area where Sarah, Cornell, and Ben sat with two uniformed men.

"These gentlemen are from the Western Massachusetts National Guard unit," Cornell said. "They demand our building – your building – on behalf of the Commonwealth." Cornell rolled his eyes when he said that.

The officer in charge didn't look amused. "Under a state of emergency, we have the right to commandeer property for the benefit and use of the citizens of the Commonwealth."

Cornell switched to his lawyer voice. "It's not clear that a grid failure meets the criteria for an emergency to warrant a property seizure."

The younger officer leaned his automatic weapon on the dining room table, where grains of salt from breakfast glittered in the weak sunlight. "We would rather have your cooperation," he said. "But it's not necessary."

"Your people can move over to the shelter section," the older man added, "but we need this part of the building for headquarters and troop housing. With access to your stored electricity and the photovoltaic equipment."

"But this is our *home*," Ben said. "It's our electricity."

The older man stood up. One of Myesha's handwritten flyers was sticking out of his pocket. So that's how they knew about us. "It's our job to safeguard all the citizens of the Commonwealth."

Ben stood too and he towered over the soldier. "Can you give us until tomorrow? We need time to move people. All those old folks from assisted living, you know?" He smiled his best bespectacled Dr. Seuss grin.

The officers looked at each other. "These premises must be vacated by 10:00 a.m."

After the officers left, Ben locked the door behind them. The five of us stood in a line at the front window and watched the armored vehicle drive away.

"What's our plan?" Sarah asked. "Should we start evacuating people to the shelter area?"

"I can handle this," Ben said, putting his arm around Sarah's shoulders.

She shrugged off his arm. "You owe us an explanation."

"I know. First, give me a couple of hours with Albie on the shortwave."

I gathered the stack of letters I'd written to Ruth over fifty years and brought them to the alcove. Ruth was already there, holding a thick bound journal in her lap. I mentally warned myself against hoping, against all the history stored in every cell of my body, that this time would be different. Ruth and I were incorrigible and impossible, but she was still my sister.

We started reading our old words aloud to each other. Chronologically. No interrupting, we agreed. No comments. No arguing.

After we were finished, we cried. And then we talked. About that cop and how we never knew if one of our rocks hit him. About prison. How we ruined our parents' lives. How we robbed our children of knowing each other.

"That's why I came," she said. "With the world in big trouble, I had to try to mend us."

"So despite everything," I asked her, "despite how badly things turned out, with the two of us not speaking to each other for most of our lives, would you do it again?"

"Try to stop the cops and everything?"

I nodded.

Ruth took my hand. "I think so. Would you?"

I didn't have to answer because Sarah stuck her head around the screen. "Ben wants to talk to us right away. Upstairs."

The air in Sarah and Ben's apartment smelled stale and unused. I sat next to Samuel.

"Let me back up," Ben said, "to that underground group in California."

"The anarchists?"

"Yes. I joined their group and had to promise not to tell anyone. Not even my family. Jeremy knew, because he was with me."

Samuel shook his head. "What does this have to do with the grid failure?"

Ben rubbed his face with both hands. "Our anarchist group orchestrated the grid failure. Last summer the Greenland ice sheet had record melting, and the surface mass balance was the lowest on record. We had to act. To wake people up to how critical the environmental issues are. To demonstrate the power of a small group of activists against Goliath."

My *son* did this? On purpose?

"What does crashing the grid have to do with waking people up?" Samuel asked.

"The Earth may have passed the tipping point, the point of no return. If we don't stop burning fossil fuels, we'll all be living off the grid because there will be no grid."

"If that's true, what use is any action?" Sarah asked.

"If people understand how dire things are, they'll demand political change. We have a massive online educational campaign starting tomorrow, to set out a plan."

"But isn't crashing the grid terrorism?" Samuel asked, clearly dreading the answer.

"Think of it as a dress rehearsal for the real thing. Our purpose was to offer a last chance to save our planet." Ben shrugged. "You decide."

I had no patience for his damn relativism. "I can't believe you did this on purpose. That's horrible. People could die, freeze to death or burn or starve."

"People *are* dying already, all over the world, from heat waves and fires and famine and disease and mega-storms and floods. Many more will die unless we act."

"What about us? The National Guard will take everything tomorrow," Samuel said.

"Our plan all along was for a ten-day blackout. It was never supposed to be permanent." Ben looked at each of us. "Next time, the grid failure might be real and not fixable."

I couldn't believe any of this. "So what now?" I asked.

"I just spoke with my friends in California. The power will return this afternoon."

"And in the meantime, you've been lying to all of us," Sarah said.

"I'm sorry," he said. "But secrecy is critical. We could all go to prison. We felt this was our only chance. Marches and petitions haven't worked."

I tried not to feel chastised by my son's dismissal of my life's political work. "Did you consider all the possible consequences? The collateral damage?"

"Did you?" Ben asked me, his voice soft.

The power returned that afternoon and we heard nothing more from the National Guard. The folks on dinner duty went all out to celebrate, roasting chickens and opening the final jars of last summer's blueberries for dessert.

I sat next to Ruth, cycling between confused and overjoyed and pissed off and then back to overwhelmed and relieved. Ruth and Cornell started talking about spending a month at the co-op next summer. Relief—or sugar—made us giddy.

"It's not really over, you know," Ben said at one point. He looked around the table at each of us. "Next time could be permanent."

Heads nodded, expressions serious and thoughtful. But I could tell Ben wasn't satisfied with their response. Relief and denial are strong emotions.

Sitting with my extended family, I study the steam rising from my mug. I don't know what comes next. I can't name the emotions swirling with that vapor. Relief, certainly, that the immediate danger is past. That I can begin to understand my son's work and figure out what I think about his actions. That Ruth and I are sisters again and beginning to make peace with each other.

I am afraid for the future. I look down at my mug and my finger traces the painted outline of a purple crane. Its wings are opened wide, and I let my heart crack open. Taking Ruth's hand, I think I finally understand us. Despite everything, against all odds, in a world demanding desperate actions with unknowable consequences, I admit to harboring a small glimmer of hope.

---

\* Published in *Solstice* Magazine, 2020

# Sometimes an Island
## the island · 2019 · Liz

Two weeks after her patient died, Liz opened the front door of the rental cottage to a solid white cloud. It had been dark the night before when she finally arrived at the last house on the point, after the rough ferry crossing and the slow drive groping through dense fog. In the morning, she hoped for sunlight, craved birdsong. But nothing penetrated the thick white shrouding the island.

She turned right along the cottage wall. Stone by stone her feet traced the path, guided by memory and her right hand against the wet shingles. When her outstretched left hand found the surf-smooth driftwood sculpture, she turned right again to follow the wet wall down the slope to the pottery studio.

The dust inside, equal parts clay and neglect, was almost as thick as the fog. A spider web crocheted a garbage can to the wall. The barrel was full of musty clay left by the owner. He had to put his kids through college, he told Liz the weekend before when she viewed the rental, and that wasn't going to happen on hand-thrown mugs and whimsical dog figurines. The wooden shelves were thick with grit, holding only a few potshards and a box of the small clay cones that measure kiln temperature and a small figure of a terrier, only bisque-fired, not yet glazed. Under the droopy pointed ears his expression was disappointed, or perhaps only perplexed. Liz rubbed the dog's cloak of dust on her shirt and turned to the potter's wheel.

The wheel stood in front of the window with the best view of the kiln outside, a brick sentry among wraithlike pine trees. It was an old-fashioned kickwheel like the one Liz used forty years ago in college. Someone had added an electric adapter and the owner left it for Liz. She hoped she could remember how to engage the motor. She hoped she wouldn't need it.

Liz squirmed to get comfortable on the molded plastic seat. Her first kick barely budged the heavy concrete wheel, but the second connected and sent a twister of dust into the air. She put the bisque terrier in the center of the turning metal circle and watched him twirl and dance.

In college she loved spinning clay into shapes, spent as many hours hunched over the wheel in the ceramics studio as in science labs. But med school left no room for pottery and then she married the professor who lectured on cardiac defects, ten years her senior. She became a pediatrician and joined her classmate Ernie's practice. After Alan died so young, she worked harder. So hard that when she turned eleven, their daughter Emma moved back to the island to live with Alan's parents.

Two weeks earlier in her office, Liz told Melissa's mother that a virus was causing the girl's fever. At midnight the hospital called. Melissa was dead on arrival. As Liz held the telephone, a chasm in the bedroom floor opened at her feet and she fell in. She drove to the hospital to sit with Melissa's parents and read the bacterium's signature on the small body, the delicate purple blotches blooming like poison flowers.

Maybe she couldn't have saved her. That's what Ernie said, reminding her that the disease was usually fatal, even with the best care. True. But it didn't matter. What mattered was that Liz thought it was a virus and sent her home and she was wrong and the girl died. Did she miss a small violet spot about to blossom on a freckled leg? Ernie said he wouldn't have done anything differently. But he wasn't the one. She was the one who didn't save Melissa.

"Why an island?" Ernie had asked.

"It was Alan's island. He was born there, is buried here. His family's still there, chasing lobsters and farming rocks. Emma lives there most of the time, with Alan's folks."

"You're banishing yourself," Ernie said.

"That's a little strong. Looking for clarity, maybe."

"In the fog?"

"Sometimes an island is the best place," she told him. "Nowhere to hide."

"Then why don't you stay with Emma and Alan's parents? Have a nice visit?"

She shook her head. She had no more words. Esther and Rufe were lovely people and she was endlessly grateful they had rescued Emma, but she craved solitude.

"These things happen." Ernie's voice was low and liquid. Liz had heard him use this tone with distraught parents and squalling infants.

Did she undress the girl? Examine every inch of skin, looking for the tiniest bloom of bleeding under the skin? She remembered that Melissa was the last patient of the day. A busy late summer day when everyone needed a paper signed for school. A day of poison ivy and nervous stomach aches. She remembered lifting Melissa's shirt, checking her belly for a rash, but did she completely undress her?

Liz stroked the terrier's terracotta coat. She tucked him in the breast pocket of her flannel shirt and dug ten fingers deep into the clay barrel, exhuming a gray clump. Standing at the kneading counter with both hands tentative on the mound, she strained to remember the rhythm of working the clay. Squeeze out the air bubbles. Lubricate the particles. Awaken the clay so it will dance on the wheel.

Not much of a ballet, she admitted forty minutes later. More like a wobble and a stagger. Her bones felt soft as she climbed around the corner of the house, pausing to admire a russet butterfly on the driftwood statue. Behind the butterfly the fog retreated. Sunlight glinted on the water like a tribe of Tinkerbells.

Over the next few weeks, the air cooled, and the fog came less often. A new breeze teased the crisp leaves into spirals and whorls of color and her fingers relearned the clay. Her fingers had always been the best of her, up to the challenge of French-braiding Emma's rowdy hair or palpating an infant's belly. They remembered how to shape the clay, but the flawless bowls drying on the shelves brought little joy. She stared at her fingers and asked them to point her in the right direction.

She visited Emma and Alan's parents several times. Emma seemed to thrive living with her grandparents but Liz felt lonelier in their brisket and sweet potato company than at the rental with the bisque terrier. A silent companion, he watched her from the shelf in the studio, from the kitchen table. Should she glaze and fire his fragile form? She was reluctant to change him in any way.

It was noon on an undecided autumn day—brisk and sunny one moment, damp and chilly the next. Liz slumped at the wheel and stared through the window to the water's edge. Low tide undressed the shoreline, exposing silt-colored mussel shells, plastic twisties, and cloudy shards of glass tangled in the yellow-brown seaweed. A heron stood frozen, its beak motionless inches from the muck.

Liz decided to quit early for a picnic lunch at Sunset Rock. She packed a sandwich, slipped a jacket over clay-crusted overalls, and settled the terrier in her jacket pocket. Walking through sea grass and across the one-lane bridge over Sleepy Simon Creek, she nodded greetings to a group of sunflowers clustered like teenage girls posing for a basketball team photograph.

She chose a sunny spot on the sloping slab of granite connecting sky to sea. Repositioning the terrier in her breast pocket so he faced the whitecaps, she bit into a cheese-and-mustard sandwich and watched people picnicking on the far side of the rock. A gray-haired woman sat alone, staring out at the bay. Three adults passed around a steaming thermos. Two boys in sweatshirts and blue jeans hurdled tidal pools and crevasses, slapping their baseball caps together in the air over their heads to celebrate each leap.

"Kee-kee-kee-kee-kee." Liz leaned back to watch the flattened 'M' wings of the osprey. When it disappeared, she exhaled a cloud of fog and let her mind roam behind her eyelids.

"Mama!"

The boy tumbled then somersaulted then bounced on stone and finally slid to a stop near the rock edge. The adults stumbled down the slippery rock to the motionless form, his sweatshirt a startling red against the white stone and white skin. A woman stopped to pick up the fallen baseball cap and clasp it to her chest.

"Don't move him. Call for an ambulance," Liz called over the howl of the ocean. The boy was wedged in a crack in the granite slab, his right arm sprawled out on the stone, almost graceful in line. A man helped Liz slide him to a flat area. Her thumbs found the notch of his lower jaw and lifted. No whoosh of air on her cheek. No stir of his chest, no beat of life in the tender valley of his neck.

Liz found her fingers, her fingers found the landmarks, and they remembered the rhythm of the rescue. The pounding of her heartbeat and the cadence of the counting muted the ocean. Then the island ambulance crew was there, strapping the backboard and collar in place and taking over the synchronized drill. The boy now had a faint heartbeat and the waves thundered again.

Rooted at the chasm in the granite, Liz watched the procession climb the stone slope to the road. One man slipped and the stretcher jerked and a small leg dangled. A man held the boy's hand where it was secured on the stretcher. The mother still clutched the baseball cap and guarded his other side while the paramedics maneuvered over the rocks. The mother turned to Liz and pressed her free hand to her heart.

Liz saw the boy's blue jeans. Like the ones Melissa wore, with strawberries embroidered on the cuffs. The jeans she didn't take off. The legs she didn't examine.

The rising tide shimmered at the edges of her vision. Liz removed the bisque terrier from her pocket. His tail was broken. She kissed his muzzle and placed him carefully on the glistening rock, on the brink of the small fissure, before climbing the rocks to the road.

She didn't see the gray-haired woman stop on her way up the jumble of stones. Didn't see Bertie pick up the clay terrier and put it in her pocket.

# Signs that Lie
## the island · 2020 · Bertie, Tutu

I know I'm not dead yet because I hear Cousin Tutu nattering on the phone propped on the hospital bedside table. That's to keep me company since this damned virus has done away with visiting hours. I can tell it's Tutu from her whiny voice—don't even have to open my eyes, which is lucky because I couldn't before when I tried to thank the aide for straightening my left foot that slipped out of the foam bootie and my heel was aching. It must be morning. There's a blue light leaching through my eyelids, aqua almost, like swimming underwater looking up at the sun. Could be some otherworldly glow but I doubt it. Most likely the nurse left the blue plastic ventilator tubing draped across my face again. She's young, doesn't think there's anyone home in here. I can't hear the squish-squeak of her bootie-covered shoes so she must have left the room. Just me and Tutu here now and she's talking to someone in the room with her, talking about me as if I'm already gone.

As Louise lowered herself into the other porch chair, Tutu pointed to the phone leaning against the teapot with a knitting needle, not missing a stitch.

"No change," Tutu said. "She's totally out of it. The nurse turned on FaceTime for a few minutes so I could see her, but she's buried in ugly tubes and machines so I asked her to put it back on just audio, not that Bertie knows what's happening. Poor Bertie."

"Poor Bertie," Louise repeated.

It drove Tutu crazy when her sister repeated her words, but she'd been doing it for six decades and probably wouldn't stop now.

"Such a crying shame," Louise added.

Her sister probably wouldn't give up her use of clichés either, but Tutu reminded herself to be nice, to not give voice to the unkind thoughts in her head. They all knew that Bertie's lifestyle—call it oddball if you wanted to be kind, but risky and even profligate if accuracy was your thing—put her at risk for all sorts of bad things and so it was no big surprise she got the virus. Tutu didn't say it, but she thought it and maybe Louise did too. Through the phone, the hospital room was quiet except for the shush of the ventilator. Tutu's porch was quiet too, just the clink of her metal knitting needles and the low sound of the ferry horn in the distance. It was a sad sound and Tutu didn't know what was sadder—that Bertie was dying alone in that hospital down in New York City or Tutu was stuck on a Maine island with Louise for company. But what did Bertie expect, after living her life like that, scattered all over the place with no thought about what was left of her family?

Tutu broke the silence. "Breaks my heart that Bertie will miss Annette's wedding." She dabbed her eye with Matt's faded plaid hanky, soft from many washings.

Louise's voice got syrupy. "Oy, to miss her girl's wedding. That's the worst thing, especially since Annette took her own sweet time settling down."

Tutu finished the row and glanced at the smartphone. Such a cute little device. Why did she resist it all these years? Good thing Nathan gave it to her for her birthday, just in time for Bertie's mess. Such a good son.

"The worst, Weez? Dying before her time is worse luck." Tutu rarely agreed with anyone else's opinions and certainly not her sister's.

Louise's voice turned shrill, and she shook her head hard enough to bounce the lacquered gray curls that proved Louise was sneaking off to the salon despite the mandated closures. "No. Before a woman dies, she should see her children's weddings and her grandchildren's bar mitzvahs."

*Sometimes an Island*

"And what about my Matt?" Tutu skewered the ball of yarn with the empty needle and let it fall into the straw basket at her feet. "May his memory be for a blessing. He won't see the wedding either, or even meet his grandchildren."

"It's worse for a mother," Louise insisted, but her sentence trailed off into silent acknowledgement that Tutu won the point.

Besting Louise was a small victory. Her sister could never stay the course in an argument. That's why she always lost them. That, and the fact that she wasn't that swift in the smarts department. Now Bertie was smart, Tutu had to give her that. Too smart for her own good most of the time. And where did it get her? Maybe having a daughter out of wedlock wasn't such a big deal in those fancy places Bertie had lived, dragging little Annette right along with her, but it wasn't done in Maine, especially on their island.

But this time, Louise wasn't giving up entirely. "Tell her, Tutu. Tell Bertie about the engagement. Think about how much she's losing. At least she should know the news."

Tutu scraped her chair closer to the phone and frowned. She felt silly talking to someone who wasn't really there. To someone she hadn't liked much when she *was* there. Someone who currently resembled a human pincushion for needles and tubes and all sorts of unpleasant medical gadgetry.

Still, Tutu considered herself a woman who performed her duty without shirking, so she leaned forward and spoke loudly at the phone. "Bertie, this is Tutu. I don't know if you can hear me, but I wanted you to know that Nathan proposed to Annette last night. They're getting married. Your Annette and my Nathan!"

*There's nothing wrong with my ears, you dim dodo. I just can't talk with this garden hose shoved down my throat. I heard you before, talking to your dimmer sister. Imagine my baby getting married and oh I know she's not a baby. Too bad I didn't hear the news from Annette herself, that's probably why she called last night but I couldn't talk and the nurse hung up. Annette doesn't talk to me about men, especially not since last fall when we met for a long weekend on the island, last fall when we could still travel, and she mentioned she was seeing Nathan and I begged her not to.*

"Why don't you like Nathan?" she had asked.

"He's your first cousin," I said. Not exactly true, but close enough.

"So? That's legal in Maine, if you show proof of genetic counseling."

"Trust me on this one." I had wondered briefly why Annette researched the law on cousin marriage if they were just dating. But not having a father had always made Annette intensely curious about the shape of other people's families.

We had been picking our path through broken shells and seaweed strewn across the rocky shore, trying to keep our sneakers dry. The island was still home, even though neither one of us had lived there in decades. I tried living there after Father died and left me the farmhouse, but I felt stifled and split after a few months, renting out the old place.

"It's no good, you and Nathan," I repeated.

"You just can't stand the idea of being in-laws with Tutu," Annette said with a laugh. "Don't worry. We're just dating. Anyway, I'm too old to have a baby."

If Annette had persisted, I supposed I could have dodged the real issue by saying something general and clinical about the dangerously small gene pool shared by the two dozen families on Saperstein Neck, all those cousins. But she never mentioned Nathan again so I didn't have to lie. I had always hoped she would find a lover to bring fresh bloodlines to the family DNA, though she's now past childbearing in any case. Wait until you've got a good reason to marry, that's what I taught my girl though I guess I can't blame her if she ignored my advice since what did I know? I let the right guy get away. Matt is three years dead and Tutu never had a clue about us.

Tutu had the marriage license but I had the best of Matt. Pilfered days of trekking together along Hurricane Ridge, water bags looped around our belts and sloshing with every step or following the Tuli Elk to the end of Point Reyes, adoring them from far away so they wouldn't catch our scent and bolt, times when Tutu thought Matt was seeing clients in Marin County or Seattle. Stopping to eat stale baguettes and oily sardines from a can with a pull-off top. Taking time to explore small off-trail clearings, perfectly sized for two bodies.

And that time in cowboy country where I was completely myself in the turtle shell of some old Chevy, stopping with Matt at every historic marker with their false promises. On our first secret trip together, we stopped at a used book barn in a barren northeast corner *of Arizona and found a dusty book about roadside monuments and how they lie. We read every word aloud to each other, laughing at each exaggerated local hero, kissing after every overwritten account, in our green canvas tent with the rainstorm outside making incongruous deep mud that we slopped through to the latrine.*

*Slosh. Squish. The nurse is back with the irregular cadence of her footsteps like she limps a little from an old injury to hip or foot. Plus the rustle and crinkle of all the protective equipment, extra gloves and gowns and shields and foot coverings.*

The nurse picked up Bertie's cell phone and spoke into it, her voice muffled by her mask. "I have to check her vitals and suction her tube, all that stuff, so I'm going to turn this off for now. Do you want me to call you back when I'm done?"

"How's she doing?" Tutu asked.

"Not well," the nurse said. "Her heart and kidneys are failing. Her lungs are terribly stiff so it's getting harder for the machine to breathe for her."

"Because of the virus?"

"Probably," the nurse said. "But her heart wasn't in great shape to begin with."

"Can she hear me, understand what I'm saying?"

"We think that hearing is the last sense to go. And the sound of your voice will comfort her, even if she doesn't understand your words."

"Please tell her Tutu and Louise are here, praying for her. And tell her not to worry. I'll call the Rabbi about burial arrangements."

*What a witch Tutu is, as if she doesn't know exactly what I think of funerals. I've always told the family I want no service, just cremation and my ashes tossed off Sunset Rock during the most glorious explosion of colors the island can produce. Not that I'd expect Tutu to trudge up that rocky path. This is precisely what I'd expect of Tutu, letting me know that she plans to smother me underground for revenge. I can't imagine what Matt saw in her besides her looks and those didn't last long. When he kissed me goodbye at the ferry the morning I left the island for nursing school, he and I had an understanding and then something changed and he stopped writing and then he married her. I never did ask him why. Too proud for my own good is what Father always said. When I heard about their engagement I headed west after graduation instead of home. I didn't count the months but when Father wrote me about Nathan's birth, I had my answer.*

*What kind of name is Tutu for a grown woman anyway? One of those terminally cutesy names with a no-doubt embarrassing story behind it that I know I've heard a thousand times and I was probably there when she got the name but I can't make myself remember it and who cares anyway? She's pear-shaped now, nothing suggesting the ballerina—trust me on that—and I don't need to open my eyes to confirm. Young or old she was never the right person for my Matt and you can trust me on that too.*

*Matt and I were best buddies as kids, riding our bikes on the dirt roads and rocky trails out on Saperstein Neck—Jew Neck the kids at school called it. One time we must have been ten or eleven and we sprawled on the warm rocks overlooking Terry Cove eating our bologna sandwiches and arguing.*

*I insisted I was a boy. "Bertie's a boy's name, isn't it?" I said as if that proved it.*

*"No way, you're no boy." Matt had freckles then, too many to count in the summer when arithmetic was optional. "Boys have balls," he said.*

*"I've got 'em," I insisted even though I had no clue what kind of balls he meant.*

*He laughed and called me Ballsy and the name stuck. When we were sixteen he whispered that name into my ear and the sound was electric. We wrestled and painted each other with squished ripe blueberries on our new skin then raced naked into the icy water of the cove. On a mattress of weather-softened pine needles sheltered by a nest of rocks we tasted each other's sweat, mouths rearticulating familiar bodies. Years later when we met again in the desert, our sex still smelled like decaying leaves and sodden ocean air and blueberries.*

*But I still didn't have the balls to tell anyone about us.*

*There were so many times I wanted to tell Tutu just to see her stuck-up face crumple and fall apart. Like at Matt's funeral when she was the weeping widow but I was the one truly bereft. Mostly I* wanted to tell Annette. I almost did, that time at the cove when she said she was dating Nathan. I was never ashamed about Matt, not even when I got pregnant on one of his visits and decided to have the baby but I never told a soul who her father was. One night at supper, visiting Father on the island when Annette was an infant, he asked about it in his offhand academic way and I know he suspected but Matt had begged me never to tell anyone about us so I didn't. I let everyone think Annette's father was the California novelist lover I invented to keep my pride when Matt wouldn't leave Tutu. In the brief private moment I had alone with him before he died, I leaned over his curtained ICU bed, kissed his closed eyelids and whispered that Annette was his.

Now it's me in the ICU bed and can't even open my eyes but I don't need them to see what's happening. This was my world for almost forty years but I'm supposed to be the one taking care of the patient, straightening the covers and soothing the pain and minding the machines that keep people alive. How did I get this assignment anyway? I'm not crazy about this. I prefer being busy, being in charge and making decisions like a stroke of flashing lightning and this isn't my style—lying here with nothing to do except remember, as if there's unfinished business if I believed in that psychobabble. Memories interrupted only by Tutu on the phone and the nurse not telling me anything and the occasional twinge of the yellow snake biting its way between my legs. Not much pain thanks to the morphine and whatever else they're pumping into my veins. Once— maybe it was last night or the one before I can't be sure because time doesn't follow the rules of seconds minutes hours days anymore—my chest hurt so bad and I must've moaned because there were voices and then I guess a bolus of morphine. A rush and I hovered for hours and now I'm still suspended in and out of clouds but now the clouds are inside and I'm somehow floating on them.


Tutu picked up the phone and it was the nurse again with video. Her stethoscope was on Bertie's chest and then she gazed at Tutu over the top of her mask through the plastic face shield. "It won't be long now. Does she have other family I should call?"

"Her daughter's stuck in London," Tutu said. "There are no flights. I tried calling her a while ago and left a message."

The nurse hung the stethoscope on the IV pole and adjusted a knob on one of the machines. The hilly green line jiggled and jerked before resuming its slow wandering across the darker screen. "Anyone else I could notify?" she asked again.

"There's just me," Tutu said. "Her lifelong pal and cousin."

Tutu opened her garden magazine and ran her index finger down the table of contents. It was unkind, she knew, but she felt a small, grim satisfaction that Bertie was dying alone and Annette wouldn't call back in time and Louise had wandered off down the lane to her own house. Bertie thought she was so smart, smarter than anyone in the world except maybe her egghead father. But really, how stupid did she think Tutu was?

*Tutu never did know anything about Matt and me. She rarely paid any attention to me except to look down her nose at my profession. "I don't know how you can stand those sick people," she would say. "Such ugly work." She must have said it a thousand times.*

*Being a nurse was never ugly to me. I liked the chaos and disorder of it. People think it's dirty work but that never bothered me either. I loved the awful intimacy of the body's hidden crevasses and secret untetherings. It was the perfect job for a woman who gets antsy staying any one place more than a season or two and I wandered from Knott County, Kentucky to Carpentaria, California, even a few months at the V.A. near San Juan in Puerto Rico. The little community hospital near the copper mines up by Globe, Arizona was the best and that's where Matt found me again more than a decade after he dumped me. I had been there two years exploring the desert on my days off when Matt came to Phoenix for a meeting and called me up—just for old time's sake, he said.*

*There was something about that land, creepy as it was, that kept me from moving on. The open pit mining scarred the earth and used her up like an old person's body. Raw gravel bubbled up from the gouges, skin baked dry and hard for empty miles. I'm no tree-hugger but that place, the barrenness of it, gave me the shivers.*

*Father begged me to come back to live with him on the island. But the isolation wasn't for me. He didn't understand my wanderlust and he didn't want me to be a nurse. Our people left Europe to get away from all the dying, he said. I was raised to be a thinker like him, fogged*

## Sometimes an Island

in half the year on an island with 700 people and six times that many books in his library. But that life wasn't for me. "So fine, be a teacher," he said, "if you must have a career other than thinking. Teaching is more tidy."

Once my father was gone, Esther was the only island person I missed, the only one I spent time with when I was there last year. Somehow I knew it would be my final visit to the island, so I said goodbye to the places I love, like Sunset Rock. It felt final, as I watched Esther's daughter-in-law save a boy's life. She left a little clay dog behind and I gave it to Esther.

No, Father didn't understand that it was the mess I liked. The jumble and chaos called to me even when I was retired and living outside Phoenix so when the virus exploded in Queens I responded to the call for health care workers and went back to work.

"She isn't responding," the nurse told Tutu. "Her lungs are consolidated and we have nothing more to offer. She's making clots all over her body and her organs are giving up." She pointed the phone to the monitor, where green spikes lengthened, unfolding in slow loops across the screen.

Tutu texted Louise. *I think she's dying. It's creepy being here with her.*

*Did you tell her about Annette?* Louise texted back.

*Yes, but I don't think she understood.* Tutu reached down to touch the soft green yarn, rub the silky strands between her fingers. Why wasn't Louise here to support her? She and Louise had never discussed the rumors, but her sister must have heard them too. Being alone with Bertie like this was spooky, even if Bertie didn't understand.

I understand just fine but right now I'm more interested in remembering that little hospital in Winkelman, Arizona halfway between the state prison with all the signs along the road warning you not to stop for hitchhikers and the mine. That's the place I lived when I found out I was pregnant with Annette and when I learned the limits of Matt's courage.

They opened that mine in 1914 and for decades local kids played *in the leftover piles of black shag. No one knew it was poison not even the mine owner until his son got sick. The ward was slow the night he died and his parents tried to nap for a couple of hours, holding each other on the sofa in the lounge. I cuddled my patient in the rocking chair on the children's ward, hugging close my new knowledge that I was pregnant and rocking that little boy and grieving for all of us.*

*Not so ballsy any more, was I? I still moved around but not as often and I never loved Matt again except as a cousin. I chose jobs based on availability of onsite childcare and how good the schools were but I still loved the work especially the emergency rooms and ICUs, titrating cardiac meds and keeping the interns from making deadly mistakes and troubleshooting the ventilators and monitoring equipment.*

*What's that shrieking noise? Sounds like a cardiac alarm like someone is in trouble and I'm trained to help. I know what to do but nothing is in the right place and where's the crash cart and what's going on and who's my patient? I can't remember my assignment this has never happened before. The alarm keeps ringing and it sounds like screaming who is screaming where's the alarm silence button?*

"What's that awful noise?" Tutu yelled at the nurse, but the nurse bent over Bertie and then smacked a large red button on the wall with the flat palm of her hand, adding another siren to the wailing and howling.

"Have to hang up now," the nurse told Tutu as she peeled open a plastic package, offering a gooey blue pad to a tall woman holding small ping-pong paddles.

"What's happening?" Tutu screeched, wishing for even Louise's company.

"Charging," the tall woman called out.

Tutu spoke loudly into the phone. "Bertie, they're making me leave. But don't worry. I'll take good care of Annette and Nathan. They'll be so happy together. And one more thing, Bertie. I never said a word to anyone, but I knew about you and Matt. Always knew."

Tutu nestled the silent phone in her yarn basket, noting that it needed a charge. For a brief, generous moment, she felt sad that Bertie would miss the wedding. Nathan and Annette planned an autumn wedding on the rocky north point of Saperstein Neck. It was their family's favorite ceremony spot, the grove of scrub pines and wild blueberry bushes overlooking Terry Cove. Tutu could picture the glorious day, the sparkly early afternoon once the sun burned the fog from their beloved island.

# Under the Huppa
## the island · 2021 · Mary

It's the perfect setting for a wedding. We've used this clearing overlooking Terry Cove for many rites of passage, weather-permitting, even before virus-mandated outdoor gatherings. Funerals, once a Bat Mitzvah, but mostly weddings. Last October for Annette and Nathan and today for Laura and Elijah's big day. Summertime on the island is at its most spectacular—lush and verdant, with a backdrop of rocky coastline and white-capped waves. Puffy clouds and just enough breeze to make the ferns dance and caress the skin of aunts and uncles and cousins sitting in rows of rented chairs. Still, our more close-minded relatives are less than thrilled with today's celebration. A few pursed-lip expressions follow Elijah's parents as we take our seats after walking the young people to the huppa.

Standing under the fabric canopy fluttering in the breeze, the bride is blue-eyed with an olive complexion like her mom, Ruby. Like me, her grandmother. She's visibly pregnant, but I'm so happy for her I don't even care. Her groom is dark and has dreadlocks, unusual for maritime Maine, and I don't mind about that either. It doesn't matter that the rabbi Laura brought up from Boston is a woman with a purple crew cut. I like how she smiles at my Laura and her Elijah. I love how they look at each other.

If only Ruby were here, it would be a perfect day.

I scan the small crowd again. Would I even recognize my

daughter after all these years? Would her hair be gray? Women in our family tend to gray early. Die early, too. My braid was steel gray by the time I was forty, though I blame that on the troubles with Ruby. Laura and Elijah stomp the cloth-wrapped wineglass and the sharp crack of glass breaking snags my attention back to the present. The raucous chorus of "Mazel Tov" lifts into the sun-dappled air. Brushing a beaded huppa tassel from her face, the rabbi puts her arms around Laura and Elijah and whispers something that makes Elijah laugh and Laura blush. Laura throws the bouquet right to her cousin Melissa, who leaps up and grabs it mid-flight.

Laura grins at Melissa at the success of their plan and I hide my smile. Not that Melissa and her Sally would do a Terry Cove wedding. The family is already stretched to the limits of tolerance by Elijah's color and Laura's pregnancy. I ignore the few folks who frown our way. For me, the baby is a promise to a better future. Is it racist of me to love her imagined skin color? I'm glad Caleb had a chance to meet Elijah before the strokes finally got him. Too bad he won't meet his great-grandbaby. No, maybe it's for the better. I know it would bother him, his granddaughter marrying a Black person. When he met Elijah a few years ago, Caleb tried not to let his prejudice show, but I could tell.

I wonder what Ruby would think.

Laura and Elijah didn't want a formal receiving line. Formal anything, really, as you can tell from their matching African print finery—Elijah's dashiki and Laura's sundress, gathered under the bust to make room for her baby bulge. But habit is strong, and the guests mingle into a free-form queue moving toward the newlyweds, Elijah's handsome parents, and me. Just beyond us, card tables with flowered tablecloths offer cake and champagne. I introduce each guest to Elijah's parents, with a word or two of how we're related. Dwayne smiles and shakes hands; Aretha offers a few words of welcome, stoops to greet a small child, graciously accepts an embrace.

As usual, Tutu and her sister Louise are first in line, with Tutu's son Nathan and his new wife Annette. Their wedding last autumn was easily the most fraught family event you could imagine, with Annette mourning her mom. Bertie died of the virus, caught while working in a hospital down in New York City. Everyone knew that Nathan and Annette shared a biological father, but no one spoke of it. Bertie thought she took that secret to the grave, but secrets rarely stay hidden on this island.

An osprey rides the air currents above, adding kee-kee-kee to the chatter of the festivities. I slip away until I'm soaring with the bird, looking down at my own wedding to Caleb in this clearing forty-five years ago. We were so young and hopeful, with everything ahead of us. Sometimes the long-ago past is more real than now and returning takes concentration.

Aretha must notice me floating. She takes my hand, ignoring how it trembles. She squeezes. Right now, anything I say will bring tears, so I squeeze back without a word. This marriage must be even more peculiar for her—her only son marrying into a family of Eastern European Jewish immigrants who populated a rocky peninsula on an island in the middle of Penobscot Bay well over a century ago and pretty much stayed there, generation after generation.

Aretha must've read my mind. "You know, Mary, that this isn't what I imagined for our boy," she says quietly. "But Laura is lovely and they are so happy."

"Our family must be so strange for you."

"Unusual," she admits. "You're Laura's grandmother and you're a year younger than me. But everyone," she hesitates, "*almost* everyone has been so kind."

I think about the pursed lip expressions. Of course she saw them. "I'm sorry."

"A few disagreeable looks." She shrugs. "Par for the course. I've never been to Maine before. It's gorgeous."

"And awfully white."

"Yes."

Elijah and his parents arrived on the island a week ago so we could prepare together for the wedding. The logistics were part of the challenge, lugging card tables and chairs and food up the twisty path from the road to this spectacular site overlooking the bay. Getting comfortable with each other was trickier, but that was happening too, bit by bit.

Mostly, we'd needed time to make the huppa.

I explained my idea to Aretha on the phone three months ago. It was our first conversation, a combination get-to-know-each-other talk and to begin planning the young people's wedding. Aretha made me feel comfortable right away.

"We love Laura," Aretha said. "Dwayne and I can't imagine a better partner for our son. How can I help with the wedding plans?"

"Our family has a tradition of sewing a huppa," I said. "One that's unique to each couple."

"That's the canopy the couple stand under for the ceremony?" Aretha asked.

"Uh huh. It's usually handmade, from cloth that has meaning to the couple and families, symbolizing the home they will make together." I hesitated, trying to picture Elijah's mother, whom I'd never met, sitting with me on the grungy plaid sofa piecing together two family legacies into something new. "I have a prayer shawl that my great-grandparents brought over from the old country. If you have some fabric with significance to your family, we could stitch them together."

"I love the idea," Aretha said. "And I know just the cloth to contribute." Then she hesitated. "Can we do that? Is it kosher? Well, not kosher, but you know what I mean. Is it allowed?"

I laughed. "The only rule I follow is that the huppa is a temporary structure made by human hands. We're not much for religion or tradition in this family."

Aretha offered kente cloth, a family heirloom from Ghana. When we placed it on the dining room table next to the tattered prayer shawl, it looked odd, for sure, but Aretha and I smiled at each other. We found it beautiful, and Laura and Elijah agreed. While Laura hiked the island with Elijah and Dwayne, Aretha and I hand-sewed the pieces together and shared passed-down family stories of the old countries. Of tyranny, of immigration, of assimilation, sometimes reluctance, sometimes ugliness and always hope. We strung beads and remembrances on silken cords to hang from the cloth—Elijah's battered Rock 'Em Sock 'Em Robot and a mangy Furby, a slinky and several neon-haired trolls from Laura's collection. We laughed over stories of our offsprings' childhoods and growing-up years. My memories are often scrambled these days, but the lost endings and garbled timelines didn't seem to faze Aretha.

Last night, after the others went up to bed, Aretha and I finished sewing and celebrated with a glass of wine. I swallowed my shame and told her about Laura's early life.

"Ruby was thirteen," I whispered. "And so wild. She refused to name the father, except to say it was a boy she knew. By the time she told us, it was too late to do anything."

"Oh, Mary," Aretha said. "That must have been so hard."

"When Laura was three, Ruby abandoned her girl, unable to face single teen motherhood living with her parents on an isolated island. Caleb and I tried to do a better job raising our granddaughter than we did with our daughter."

"You did the best you could," Aretha added. Not a stick of judgment in her voice. I loved her for that.

I confessed that I'd been trying to track Ruby on social media the past few years, with the technological help of my cousin Sadie's niece, Emma. Caleb would have been furious. We argued about it while he was alive, and he was adamant that Ruby had made her bed and must lie in it.

"Think of Laura," Caleb would say.

"I am," was my rote answer.

"Ruby is dead and gone," Caleb had insisted. "To me, anyway."

But Caleb was gone now and besides, we'd had no response on social media. Nothing, no sign of her anywhere. Could Ruby have changed her name?

"You must really miss her," Aretha said.

I pour more wine, too embarrassed to admit that Emma and I had written dozens of messages to Ruby, sent them out into what Emma called cyberspace, inviting her to today's celebration. I wish I could share that with Aretha, and my diagnosis too, but I didn't want anything sad to shadow our celebration of Laura and Elijah.

Again, I cajole my brain back to here and now. To the wedding and Aretha and the birds and the sky and the ferns and the sea. Whether Ruby shows up or not, Laura looks so happy and comfortable with herself, so I guess Caleb and I did all right by her. I could die happy. Though of course I want to live for this new life she and Elijah are making together. I want to love this baby.

The next guests finish wishing Laura and Elijah all the best in life and turn to me. My cousin Esther, supported by a cane on one side and her granddaughter Emma on the other.

"Rufe is too ill to attend," Esther says. "The next time we're here will probably be for his funeral."

Esther and I share a long embrace, a silent moment. I don't tell her that my funeral won't be long after his.

Emma tries to lighten the mood. "Did you see that Sadie's here today, with her son and his Brooklyn family?" She calls to a group of adults and children looking at the ocean. Sadie turns and blows kisses in my direction. Sadie has been my best friend forever. I've been miffed at her for moving off-island, to her homestead in the woods, and trying to get everyone else to join them there. Guess I'd better start working on forgiving her before it's too late.

I tear up again, thinking about how bereft we are when family moves away. About losing those we love. Me losing Caleb. Esther preparing to lose Rufe. Ruby, who may not be dead but is lost to me. How moments of joy are so often shadowed by sorrow. I look around this place, this green and joyful rocky outcropping residing at the intersection of then and now, of native mountain laurel in full bloom and bittersweet vines, invasive and toxic.

My first vivid memory of Terry Cove was my grandfather's funeral. He immigrated to this island a century ago with two friends and a 10-year-old girl, fleeing the pogroms in their small village near Odessa, leaving everything behind. He hoped to farm and raise a family, but finding granite instead of topsoil, he became a stonecutter. He didn't have much use for organized religion and wanted to be buried here, in his favorite place on the island, starting the Terry Cove tradition. That November day, the trees were bare, and frost crunched underfoot. I was six. Sadie was eight. The two of us built fairy houses from twigs and leaves and pinecones during the ceremony. Lifelong cousin-friends.

I force myself back to now. "How's Sadie's visit going?" I ask Esther.

Esther frowns and I pat her hand. Sadie bought land way inland after that chunk of Greenland fell into the sea a couple of years ago, and she's trying to gather the extended relatives at the Homestead—that's what they call it. Sadie is convinced that half our island will be underwater soon, and maybe she's right. Yes, she's probably right, and while I'm honored to be invited to join Sadie's party, I'll stay home and go down with my island. I think about Grandpa, leaving all his people behind in Europe to escape to a better life, and now his descendants are fleeing again, from another man-made danger.

And I think about his mother, my great-grandmother, back in Europe. Heartbroken but hoping her son would survive in the new world. She probably didn't live long either, given what was coming her way. I glance over at Laura, stroking her belly as she laughs at something a cousin said, and a fist of gratitude squeezes my heart.

"If only Sadie would bring her family home," Esther says quietly. "This is where we all belong."

"We'll go visit them in a few weeks, as soon as Rufe can make the trip," Emma promises. "They're not moving back here, Bubbe."

I turn to introduce Esther and Emma to Elijah's parents. Are they my in-laws or is there another word for it? Aretha and I talked about this last night. "Co-in-laws?" she offered. We needed a legitimate word for this new connection and settled on the Yiddish term machatunim.

While Esther charms Aretha and Dwayne, Emma pulls me aside. Emma is an old soul, still in her teens but comfortable with my generation. She whispers, "Any word from Ruby?"

I shake my head. I'm not sure if I'm disappointed or relieved. I don't tell her that yesterday I called the Rockland-based detective in charge of Ruby's missing person case 28 years earlier. Nothing new, he said, trying and failing to keep the annoyance out of his voice. I don't tell her that I've seen Ruby in my dreams, a ghost in the fog.

The line snakes forward, everyone hugging and relaxing into the social part of the occasion, lubricated by champagne in plastic flutes. Laughter erupts from a gaggle of girls near the huppa, and I recognize Sadie's granddaughter, Tillie. She must be about sixteen. Ruby's age when she couldn't stand it any longer and snuck out of the house, taking the early ferry out of our lives.

Other than Laura, all I have left of Ruby is a lopsided ashtray she made in school as a Mother's Day gift and a photo in our family album, a group of 12- and 13-year-olds from her school class, the year she got pregnant. I think about those other children; some of them are celebrating with us today and they're middle-aged. In her absence, in my heart, Ruby hasn't aged at all.

Finally, the last guests move to the refreshment table. Laura slips away from her beloved for a moment to hug me. "Thank you," she whispers.

I adore my granddaughter. She is a young woman, but I see a three-year-old just abandoned by her mother.

Aretha and I hang back as everyone else joins Laura and Elijah to do that silly thing with the wedding cake, which is half chocolate and half vanilla. "Like your baby?" I had asked. Laura laughed. "No, because some people like chocolate and some don't."

"She's not here?" Aretha asks.

I love that she's thinking about Ruby too. I shake my head.

"Oh, Mary. I'm sorry."

"I didn't really expect her to come."

"But you hoped."

"Yes."

Yes, I hope. And I wonder what Ruby would think of this gathering, this celebration in a homeplace that felt like prison to her? What would she think of her daughter, grown up and independent? And pregnant? How would that feel to a woman who abandoned her own daughter?

What would I say to her if she showed up?

At the edge of the rocks, I stand alone with my ghosts. This place is as holy as a secular spot can be and I want to be buried here, to forever have this view. The wind has picked up, pushing clouds across the blue. I shiver and wrap my shawl around my shoulders. My heart unfurls, but my mind is failing, my memories coated with Teflon. My hands shake constantly. I haven't shared the diagnosis, but everyone sees. Still, not one person in my family speaks of it to me.

My ghosts beckon me closer to the edge, but even my half-fuzzy brain rejects them. I push them away. Not yet. Not today. Still, before I join the others for a piece of cake, I scan the crowd again.

She might still come home, right?

# A Nesting of Stories
## the island · 2022 · Esther

At my husband's Shiva, my eyes keep returning to the nesting dolls on the mantel. They are olive-skinned with Sephardic features and black hair. Their bodies are painted a deep blood red, with tangles of leaves and vines. Each matryoshka doll has a large gold circle on the front where a pregnant womb would be, painted with a different stylized scene with ponds and bridges and deep forests and dark skies. I look at them now, and wonder where they really came from, what they have seen, what they know but won't tell me.

They stand separated, each one alone, lined up by decreasing size. From my seat on the green plaid sofa, purring cat on my lap, the dolls stare at me, urging me to do or say something. They have been silently, inexplicably, daring me since my bubbe gave them to me sixty-six years ago, in this very room.

At the time, it felt like a spectacularly poor birthday gift choice for a teenage girl who was trying to be glamorous. Today it's easier to look at them than at Rufe's worn corduroy recliner, his throne and prison during the last months of his illness. For decades the dolls have been trying to tell me something, perhaps an alternative reality about layers of living, simultaneous existences, I suppose. But when I try to think about dolls inside dolls, cycles of living and dying, worlds inside worlds, my head spins. I am grateful for my granddaughter, who interrupts my spiraling maudlin thoughts to bring me a cup of lapsang souchong and a bear claw. And herself.

"You doing okay, Bubbe Esther?" she asks.

I inhale the smoky steam and smile at Emma. When she was born, 16 years ago yesterday, I refused that title. Bubbe meant babushkas, boiled-to-death chicken, and rolled stockings, like my grandmother. But at 82, bubbe doesn't sound so insulting. I still refuse to boil chicken.

I answer Emma's question with a quarter-smile. I can't speak. I bite the inside of my cheek to prevent the tears spilling over. For something to do, I bring the bear claw to my mouth, breathe in the thick almond aroma, but can't take a bite. The cat pushes against my hand, so I let her lick the pastry.

Emma leans toward me and brushes the soft ends of her thick brown braid back and forth along the back of my hand. Braids are our special language. When she was a baby, she liked to grab my gray braid and stroke her cheek with the wisps. Emma and I have always been close. Her dad, my son Alan, moved away for college and rarely returned, but Emma spent summers with us on the island. When Alan died and Liz buried her grief in work, Emma spent more and more time living with Rufe and me. She moved here full-time when she was eleven. Such a blessing.

Son-in-law David wanders over, looking like he wishes he was out fishing, was anywhere but here. He starts to sit down on Emma's other side. When she shakes her head, he leaves without speaking, without looking at me, returning to the dining room table with its platters of comfort foods and clusters of cousins and neighbors.

*Thank you*, I nod. Emma is a treasure. Most young women would begrudge sharing their birthday with an old man's death-day, but Emma was always close with her Zayde, listening to his old country stories, not minding how the plots shifted and twisted in the retelling, how characters morphed into other versions of themselves.

One of Rufe's favorite stories was about my nesting dolls. It was fabricated in the oddly convoluted way that couples who have been together for eons appropriate each other's histories. In Rufe's story, the nesting dolls are matryoshka dolls from the town in Russia where his grandparents were born. Matryoshka means little matron, but in his version, the painted dolls represent generations of women and girls fighting against the czar, fighting for freedom for the serfs. He told Emma he grew up with those stories, each doll named for a freedom-fighter, all of them murdered, and each passing on her story to a resistance daughter nested inside her wooden body. While he talked, he rubbed his long fingers over the dolls' smooth painted faces. Sometimes the friction made his coarse black finger fur stand up with static electricity, which always made Emma laugh. "You're giving them real hair, Zayde," she would tell him.

In my story, the real story, the first time I saw the dolls they were wrapped in reused birthday tissue paper. It was 1953 and I was 16, trying to grow up fast. Bubbe Deborah's gift came with a tale, like so much of my family legacy. She said they came with her when she escaped the pogroms in her village, but that history meant little to me. She called them babushka dolls, babushka meaning old woman or grandmother, and that made more sense, since they came from her. Grandmother to mother; matron to daughter. I told Emma my story too, but I think she preferred Rufe's version.

I was too old for dolls, but for a month I played with them secretly in the closet of the room I shared with my two sisters, the only private space in our crowded multi-generation household. Each doll represented a member of my family. Father was the biggest, Mother next, then my sisters, me, and my brother. The smallest, who did not open, was the sister who was born dead when I was five.

Sixteen is a hard age to be female, and the 1950s were harder than most. I wanted to grow up, but the grown-up world was so perilous I also wanted to stay a little girl. My father was a Communist, like Rufe's uncle, Bertie's dad. Bertie and I never really got along, but we had the bond of a dangerous secret, risky even on the island. We both knew what happened to Communists who were discovered by the FBI; they were strapped in the electric chair and fried.

So I sealed my father's secret inside the smallest nesting doll who didn't open, so she couldn't be questioned about her patriotism or affiliations, and put her inside the brother doll, along with a Jewish star on a chain that Deborah hid from the Cossacks and I never took out. My brother had the same name as one of the boys whose parents were electrocuted for being Communists and Jews and maybe the name brought him bad luck because he's gone too, blown to pieces in a Vietnam jungle before he was thirty. I used to push his stroller when we walked into town to the market, until the time I steered a wheel into a deep rut, and he smashed his forehead into the gutter. After that our mother only let our sister Marga do the pushing.

Marga is the oldest. She's also the bossiest. She's here today, offering her support, she says, although I could do without. Emma tries to head her off too, but Marga ignores her and sits on the sofa next to me. I don't have the energy to get up and leave, so I look away, through the open glass-paned doors to the long slope of meadow down to the water. It's late spring, still chilly to have the doors open, but all these people in the house make the air stuffy and I hate that. I grew up in this house where the air has always been thick with relatives, living and passed on. I had no alternative when I was a kid and fighting for oxygen with siblings, parents, grandparents, all stuffed in this space.

That changed when Rufe and I got together his senior year. Growing up on Saperstein Neck, we'd known each other since kindergarten, but in an electric instant we were new. We moved to the mainland for college and Rufe's grad school and when we returned, we moved into the old farmhouse with my folks. Sadie and Alan and Rufe and I fit just fine. We loved being on the island and the air—damp and foggy—was plentiful. I could breathe. Rufe studied his precious Penobscot Bay crustaceans, and I taught seventh grade. Not by choice, but nobody else wanted the rowdy 12-year-olds. By the time I had the seniority to switch, I was embedded with the preteen troops, in all their hormonal confusion and uncomfortable honesty about the world. We took care of my parents until they passed, then I inherited the house and land. Marga resented it, of course, although she would never have left her fancy Victorian in Camden. Rufe and I moved into the biggest bedroom and the matryoshkas stood nested together on my dresser, rarely noticed in the quick tempo of our lives.

The cat jumps to the floor and wanders off. I use my cane to push up from the sofa and walk to the bay window overlooking the Sound. Still, why did Rufe have to die in spring, his favorite season? There are no curtains to block the view and we leave the waterside windows cracked open much of the year, to breathe the ocean and the faint promise of scent from the red spruce near the house. The last couple of years, her needles have become thinner. Like my hair. The tree might be dying, or maybe it's my eyes. It doesn't matter. Today I am a lone tree. Alone tree. My nesting dolls are unique too. One-of-a-kind.

*Sometimes an Island*

For years I've studied other matryoshkas. Most of them are female, with blonde or light brown hair and pink circles on their cheeks, although I've seen some stylized animals and occasional marketing attempts with television or movie figures. A travesty, no? Commonly, the dolls are painted baby blue or pink or lavender, with flower decorations, mostly roses and daisies, which are reproduced smaller and smaller on the inside dolls. My dolls are different. Less beautiful, maybe, like they have a painful past.

People are leaving now, and I am still wordless. A cousin comes by with her daughter, arms extended for an embrace. Perhaps my face reflects the purple clouds in my head because she drops her arms and blows a kiss instead. "He's better off now," she murmurs as she turns away. "May his memory be a blessing."

Rufe wasn't observant; neither of us were. Are. Were. How do you decide on verb tense when half of you is gone and half still here? Most Jews don't believe in an afterlife, but I like to imagine Rufe in the Bardo, resting a bit until he gets a new body. One with a sturdier heart, I hope. Emma hands me a hanky before I sense that my cheeks are wet.

Marga pats my hand. Why do people think that kind of touch is comforting? It reminds me that Rufe will never touch me again and I bite my cheek again. I won't cry in front of Marga, who has always taken her birth order as a mandate to rule. With our family so diminished and dispersed, Marga focuses her authority on me.

Our middle sister was the only sibling who embraced our father's political beliefs. While we were busy with our lives, she moved from Commie summer camp in the Berkshires to college activism to underground violence in her own not-so-cold war. After she went to prison and my brother flunked out of college, was drafted, went to war, and died, I wore blinders to keep the danger away. They say that many traits skip a generation and my daughter-in-law and granddaughter are climate activists, so maybe that's true. I hope so; we need their passion.

As if she hears my thoughts and disapproves of them, Marga stands up suddenly—as suddenly as an 87-year-old woman can muster—and walks to the mantel. Two by two, she picks up the painted dolls and places them on the coffee table in front of us, near my tea and uneaten bear claw. She has never forgiven our bubbe for giving them to me instead of her. She alternates between expressing her bitterness and questioning their provenance. She lines them up in order now, biggest to tiny one, then leans back against the sofa pillows.

"If they're so old, old, old," Marga asks, "how come they match our family perfectly?" The straight line of her mouth turns up slightly at one corner, pleased with her argument. "What are the chances of that?" she adds, before switching strategies. "As the oldest, I should have been the one trusted with the family legacy."

Then she leans forward and starts to nest them, placing the smallest doll with our parents' secrets into poor dead little brother.

"Don't touch them." My voice cracks.

Marga's hand freezes. She looks at me. Emma looks at me too. These are the first words I've spoken today.

"Leave them alone," I repeat, enjoying the words swelling in my mouth.

Marga clasps her hands together over her chest. She opens her mouth, then closes it.

I gather the dolls into my lap, in the folds of the black skirt borrowed from my mother's closet. I scoop them up and let them fall into the fabric with faint clunking sounds, then do it again. The cat returns, sniffs each doll in my lap, then curls up next to me.

The matryoshka principle describes object within object, person within person, idea within idea. That's what Rufe's story told us, that we're all connected in the brokenness of the world and the fixing of it. Layers of onions, bringing sharp sadness and tears and sustenance. A chain of fighters and resisters, mothers and grandmothers. And granddaughters.

For the first time in years, I nest the dolls. Dead baby sister holding secrets goes inside soldier brother, also long-gone. I'm next, holding my brother in my body, and the two of us cuddle inside our incarcerated sister. Then Marga and our parents. I twist the father doll closed. I think about Rufe and wish there were a matching doll for him.

I cradle the nesting family in my hands, rubbing my fingers across their still glossy paint. The cat purrs. I understand that it's time, and that both stories, mine and Rufe's, can be true.

Then I look at Emma. I kiss her cheek and hand her the nesting dolls.

"Happy birthday, Emma."

# Crossing
## the island · 2023 · Mary

**W**inter crossings tend to be physically rough and sparsely peopled.
That March afternoon, a dozen paying customers ride the 2:45 p.m. boat from Rockland. Wave after wave of sea spray blasts the smudged windows of the ferry. No tourists hang over the railing, binoculars swinging with the sway of the boat. Four men wearing jackets with trucking company logos sit in the small rear snack area, taking frequent swallows from bottles wrapped in wrinkled brown paper bags. A family of five plays raucous games of Hearts at the large table near the heater. Two solitary women sit at separate tables in the central seating area, bags and duffels tucked securely at their feet. One carries a sleeping toddler in a cloth sling across her chest.

Ten miles ahead, on an island in the center of Penobscot Bay, I hover over the ferry dock studying the horizon to the west. If you can't imagine the possibility of ghosts, you might want to abandon this story right now. The older I grew and the closer to death, the more I understood about ghosts. Now I am dead and I am a ghost and my funeral is tomorrow. And no, I will not be giving away any secrets about what comes next. We all sign a non-disclosure clause.

My husband passed three years ago, and my closest kin are gone as well. That leaves only my beloved granddaughter Laura and her dear little one to regret abandoning. Well, also my long-lost daughter

Ruby, of course, but she's probably already a ghost, although I haven't run into her yet. I think Laura and Leah will probably be okay but I watch over the ferry in the rough water, still unsure of my new abilities. I watch the two young women and the toddler, my kinfolk all three, promising myself not to interfere.

Laura rocks back and forth in the metal chair, which is bolted to the floor for safety. Her daughter's head finally slumps to the side and her pursed mouth makes soft snoring music, but Laura can't stop rocking yet, even though the motion mixed with the tossing of the waves makes her stomach clench and heave. She looks with longing at the other woman in the passenger area: a younger woman, barely out of her teens.

Zoe touches the brake locks on her chair a third time, satisfied that it is securely wedged under the café table. She cradles a half-mug of peppermint tea in both hands, willing it to settle her stomach against the fierce rolling of the boat and her dread at the prospect of visiting the island that made her mother so sad. When a particularly wild surge strikes the boat, the mug jerks and splatters tea onto the orange table and her lap. Zoe moans.

"Are you okay?" Laura calls. "Your face is green."

"No." Zoe dabs at the tea splotches with her scarf. "Not okay. Is the crossing always like this?"

"Often," Laura admits. "Saltines can help with nausea. I still carry them in my backpack, a memento of pregnancy."

Zoe covers her mouth with her hand. "Not a good idea," she says. She looks around the seating area. "If you come sit with me, I promise not to spill anything on you. Maybe talking will take my mind off this demented circus ride I never wanted to take in the first place."

Laura stands, toddler sleeping in the soft wrap across her chest, and walks unsteadily, hands clutching chair to chair, to Zoe's table. "Thanks. This crossing is taking awfully long, and my kid finally fell asleep, and I'm dying for some conversation that doesn't involve Daniel Tiger."

Zoe waves her hand at the empty chair. "Please join the Wild Crossing Women's Association. I'm Zoe."

"Maybe the Wild Women's Crossing Association? My name is Laura. This temporarily quiet whirling dervish is Leah."

Zoe peeks at the baby's face and smiles, ignoring the clutch of emotion in her chest.

At a particularly fierce swell-and-drop, Zoe grabs the edge of the table, then rechecks her wheelchair brakes. Laura puts a sleeve of saltines on the table in front of Zoe, who shakes her head. Laura takes a cracker and pops it whole into her mouth, then puts both arms around Leah.

"It'll be okay, Peanut," Laura murmurs, reassuring herself more than the sleeping child.

"How much longer?" Zoe asks.

Laura tilts her head. "Another 45 minutes, at least. Is this your first time going to the island?"

Zoe nods. "I hoped to never see the island."

I feel sad hearing this, but I'm not surprised. Her family had a rough time of it.

"So why are you on this godforsaken ferry going someplace you never wanted to go to?" Laura asks.

Zoe shakes her head, then nibbles on the corner of a cracker.

The women are quiet for several long seconds, interrupted by a burst of laughter from the truck drivers in the makeshift bar. The engine noise, a harsh background to the voices and the smash of the waves, suddenly cuts off.

"Uh oh," Zoe says. "That can't be good."

A long moment passes before a squeak of static over the PA system confirms her words.

The static forms into words. "This is Captain Jimmy Wilson. We got a bit of engine trouble. We'll keep you informed as our crew figures it out."

Zoe breaks the silence. "Is it my imagination or are the waves worse now, without the engine?"

"Makes sense, doesn't it?" suggests Laura. "The forward power of the ferry cut through the waves, but now we're at their mercy. Riding them as they come."

"Terrific." Zoe touches her brakes.

"The silver lining is that we have more time to get to know each other," Laura says with an exaggerated grin. "You were going to tell me what brings you to the island, Zoe. Hardly the tourist season."

"My mom's from there, but she moved to Massachusetts before I was born. Her parents died in a boating accident in a storm in these waters and Mom was devastated. She left the island as soon as she could and never returned. She called me a few days ago to say that our cousin died, and she couldn't bear to come, but would I please attend the funeral to represent our family." Zoe shrugs. "So here I am."

Laura grabs Zoe's arm. "Wait. Who's your cousin?"

"Mary. Mary Saperstein?"

Laura's face crumples. "My grandma."

Oh, at that moment I wished I could hug my sweet girl and tell her it's okay. But I'll have to hope Zoe can comfort her. And she does.

"I'm so sorry." Zoe puts her hand over Laura's. "That must mean we're related. What a coincidence!"

"Not really. Pretty much everyone on the island is related. Well, everyone on Saperstein Neck, anyway."

"What's Saperstein Neck?" Zoe asks.

"Where the Jews settled." Laura squeezes Zoe's hand, then pulls hers away. "So you're Anna's kid? The one with..."

"Spina bifida. That's me."

A massive swell grabs the ferry and tosses it into the air. Zoe's mug slides off the table, bounces on the wood plank floor and skitters to the walls. Zoe yelps and grabs the sleeve of saltines before it follows. Laura hugs her baby.

"Ticky-kicky-coin-coin," Laura whispers into her daughter's scalp.

I choke up when she says that.

"What?" Zoe asks.

"Something my grandpa and I used to say when I was scared, or unhappy. You okay?"

"Nope."

"These ferries are very stable," Laura says. "It's unpleasant, but we won't capsize."

"Thanks." Zoe groans. "Hadn't even thought of that. Just trying not to barf."

Laura smiles at Zoe. "Think about this instead. Our moms knew each other. One of the only things we have from my mother is a group photo from grade school. Seventh grade, her last year at the school. One time I got Grandma to label all the kids in the picture for me. Anna was one of them. She was a couple of grades behind Ruby, my mom."

"So then, how are we related?" Zoe asks. "I was never good at family trees."

"I think our great-grandfathers were cousins back in Europe," Laura says. "They immigrated together. You figure out what that makes us."

"No clue!" Zoe says. "I'm so sorry about your grandma."

Laura kisses Leah's hair before responding. "She wasn't just my grandma. Ruby—my mom—got pregnant at thirteen. She hated this island with a deep passion. Kinda like your mom, I guess. Anyway, one day when I was three, she just up and left. Grandma and Papa raised me. Papa died three years ago after a series of strokes. Now my grandmother, Mary. That leaves me pretty much alone in the world. Me and Peanut here."

"What about your ... partner? Boyfriend?" Zoe asks.

"Husband, but we're sort of separated. Temporarily, I think. Hope."

Zoe looks intently at the sleeping child and opens her mouth to speak.

The PA static interrupts them. "Bad news, folks. We seem to have burned out a solenoid valve and without it, we are stuck right here in the middle of the Bay. We're in communication with the Maine Ferry Authority about repairing it or getting a replacement. We'll let you know the plan when we know. Sorry for the delay."

The women look at each other. How long could it take to get a part to a boat in the middle of Penobscot Bay?

"I hope we're there in time for the funeral tomorrow," Zoe says. "Tell me about your baby. We've got lots of time."

"She's eighteen months old. Her dad Elijah and I met at the hospital in Boston where we both worked. After Leah was born, he went climate crisis crazy, to save the world for his daughter. Now he's a full-time activist, traveling all over training folks in civil disobedience, and I'm a single working mom. He's doing great work—I know that—but I married a nurse, the kindest, gentlest guy I know. This life isn't what I signed up for."

Zoe shakes her head. "That's tough, Laura. Maybe you'll work it out?"

"Sure, maybe," Laura says. "After Elijah succeeds in getting all fossil fuels outlawed. By then, if we're lucky, Boston will be under water and Leah will be changing my diapers."

She smiles at Zoe. "What about you? Do you have a sweetie?"

Zoe shrugs. "Jeremy and I have been together since I was a kid.

Literally. I met him when I was five. When he finished grad school a few years ago we moved into a co-op in western Massachusetts with a bunch of people. I really love them, but they're mostly older than us and they know who they are in the world and I'm still figuring it out. I think I'd like to have a baby, but Jeremy's scared shitless. How can we bring new life into this fucked-up planet and all, you know? Anyway, Ben, one of the guys in the co-op, was part of an anarchist group that shut down the grid a few years ago and now he's in prison and the co-op is falling apart. Jeremy, too. So everything in my life is up in the air."

Laura brings her lips to her daughter's head in a long, silent kiss. "I guess both our lives are upended because of some guy we love trying to save the world."

Zoe smiles. "I don't know about your Elijah, but I think what Ben did was a good thing. Mostly. Jeremy says that the unintended consequences get you every time."

"Sometimes I wonder about our great-grandfathers fleeing Europe and settling on the island. How brave they were, what stories they must have had of the shtetl and the journey and learning English and all. And what they had to leave behind."

Zoe shakes her head. "I don't know much about it. My mother hated talking about the island."

"I grew up with those stories, about three cousins—or best friends, depending on who's telling the story—Jacob Saperstein, David Levi, and Abel Isenfeld. They lived in a shtetl somewhere in Eastern Europe. A ghetto, pretty much. When the pogroms got bad, killing most of their families, they escaped. Jacob brought his daughter Deborah, but they were unable to rescue any other family members."

"They lost everyone else?" Zoe asks.

Nodding, Laura rubs small circles on Leah's back through the cotton of the baby carrier. "I don't know the story of how they got to the island. I asked my grandparents once and didn't get a good answer. Or maybe I've forgotten."

Hmmm. I wonder if I should have told her that story; it's not pretty. I don't remember the details, but one of the men won some land in a card game. There were accusations of cheating, but who knows. It happened more than a century ago.

"One part I do remember," Laura adds, "is how they named it

*Sometimes an Island*

Saperstein Neck. Jacob suggested they vote, the democratic way since they were in America now. And since there were two Sapersteins, him and Deborah, and just one Isenfeld and one Levi, he won the vote."

Caleb and I argued about that for decades! He was a Saperstein and I'm an Isenfeld. That wasn't democracy; it was cheating. That's what I think. It wasn't fair then and it still isn't.

But it was so long ago, and who cares?

"I always thought I'd live here again someday," Laura says. "On the island, not the ferry. I want Leah to know her people. Have a sense of history."

"Did your grandma own a house? Is it yours now?"

A wave hit the ferry and tossed it sideways. Laura grabbed the table and her daughter's sleeping body. "Yikes. Hadn't thought about that. I guess the house is mine, unless my mom shows up to claim it."

I look down at the two young women. I hadn't thought about the possibility of Ruby showing up at the funeral and claiming the house. I left it to Laura in my will. Ruby returning is highly unlikely.

Laura sighs. "What about you? Have you been curious about the island? Ever wanted to see it for yourself? Where your grandparents lived and died?"

"Funny," Zoe says. "I never think of them as my grandparents. I never knew them. And no, I never wanted to come back here. This place was poison for my mom, so that's how I think of it, too."

"That's something else we have in common. My mom hated the island too." She grins at Zoe. "Hey, where are you staying on the island?"

"The motel near the ferry terminal. Though I'm not sure how my wheelchair will manage it."

Laura grabs Zoe's hand. "Stay with me! There's plenty of room and a first floor bedroom."

Zoe shakes her head. "I couldn't do that. You'll have so much to do."

"You'd be doing me a giant favor. I've been dreading staying there alone, just me and the peanut. Please! We can talk about having babies...About Elijah and Jeremy."

Zoe nods slowly. "Thanks. I was worried about that motel."

Hovering over the turbulence, I shield my eyes from the glare on the water. I'm glad I finally told Laura the whole truth about her mother a few years ago. Long overdue. The problem with keeping secrets is that they begin to rot. To stink like dead sea creatures on the rocks. I love eavesdropping! I'm curious about their conversations to come. About loving or hating the island. No middle ground? Really, life on the island is just like anywhere else, except more so. Sometimes an island is the whole world.

Sometimes it's not enough.

If I'm being honest, I'm looking forward to my funeral tomorrow. It's a damn inconvenient setting for those who live off-island, but I don't care about that anymore. I'll see all my Saperstein Neck kin, living and long gone, a long line of ghosts marching across the ocean from a shtetl in eastern Europe, connected by blood and DNA and scar tissue.

Okay, I've given these delicious young women enough time to find each other. I wasn't afraid of dying but hated the idea that I couldn't help Laura find her way home.

The boat lurches. The motor sputters, catches, and roars.

The two women look at each other and smile. Leah squirms in the confines of the baby carrier and opens her eyes.

The captain's voice on the public address system announces that the problem is fixed. "We're back in business." Relief is loud in his voice. "We'll be at the dock in thirty minutes, give or take."

The ferry surges into the swells.

# Collateral Damage
## the co-op · 2023 · Jeremy, Sarah

### Jeremy

When the vines returned after almost a decade, they came with voices. Not loud or frightening voices but disturbing all the same. In all the times the plants came to him before, they spoke only once, when he was nine. "We have names," they said then, and he wanted to learn their names. One thing led to another, and he became a permaculture botanist.

The vines hadn't visited since college. But if the nurse practitioner who treated him back then had been correct, their appearance now could be stress-triggered. It was hard to imagine a more stressful period than the present moment. Everything was falling apart.

This time, the plants appeared when Jeremy was collecting eggs, even though that was Myesha's job. It happened pretty much the way it had before. First his fingers came alive, electric and tingling. He opened his hands and splayed his fingers in front of his face and watched his fingertips swell as buds formed and pushed and grew, finally erupting through the skin and bursting forth into green shoots with a sharp sting. He focused so completely on the sprouting stalks, the stems curling around his arms and torso, the unfurling leaves and suckermouths, that he didn't realize the sounds were vine-talk. Of course, the chickens cackled loudly like they usually did, and plant language is mostly song. The words were soft and hard to distinguish. Were they saying *feet*? What were the vines trying to tell him this time, as they grew out from and around his body, simultaneously embracing and opening him?

Once the vines started, he couldn't think about anything else, but they finally withered, and the voices faded away. He found himself collapsed in the corner of the chicken coop with the basket of eggs—miraculously unbroken—on the soiled straw next to him. He was curled into a fetal position. Ironic, since anything even vaguely embryonic was a sore topic between Zoe and him. A Rhode Island Red nestled against his hip. Myesha had insisted that chickens cuddle, and he hadn't believed her. He owed her an apology.

His first rational thought was that he should talk with Patty. She had treated him at University Health Services after the dramatic vine invasion that ended his wee-hours college radio program about imperiled plants. Patty had opened her office to him for weekly conversation. She refused to call it therapy, insisting that she wasn't a mental health specialist, but she listened and together they came up with theories and strategies. By the time he'd completed grad school, the vines had pretty much stopped coming and Patty had become a friend and then co-op family. Jeremy wondered how much her kindness to him had to do with her falling in love with Zoe's father.

Today was different though. He wasn't a kid or a college student. He was supposed to be a competent grown-up, firmly rooted in the real world. He had a partner he loved, work that engaged his brain and his heart, people who relied on him. But Zoe couldn't stop talking about her cousin and that stupid island. She wanted a baby, and he couldn't imagine bringing a child into such a broken world.

And the biggest thing was that their co-op was falling apart, and he bore some responsibility for that. If he hadn't kept Ben's secret, if he had confided in Sarah about what Ben's group was planning, maybe things wouldn't have gone so very wrong. Ben would still be here with them, running the solar array and batteries and keeping them together instead of stuck in prison as an eco-terrorist. Now it was up to the rest of them to figure out how to keep the lights on and the building heated, how to care for this family, this crazy group of people he adored. Jeremy had no time for talking vines that grew into and out of his body.

Still, he couldn't help wondering what the plants wanted from him after such a long absence.

## Sarah

I went to the rooftop looking for eggs for breakfast and found Jeremy cradling a hen in the corner of the coop. He was whispering to her, or maybe singing. Tears streaked his cheeks, which could have been from the intense chicken-poop smell, but I didn't think so. I'd found him weeping a couple of times and I knew he blamed himself for what happened with Ben. But it wasn't his fault; my husband had only himself to blame. I take that back. We were all to blame, for not paying more attention. I didn't know what Ben and his anarchist buddies were planning, but I *should* have known. I suspected that something was off, but not until it was much too late to change the trajectory of what happened.

"What's wrong?" I asked Jeremy.

He swiped the back of his hand across his eyes. "They're back."

"Them?"

"The vines. You know, the plants. With voices this time."

I didn't know Jeremy when all that happened to him, but of course I had heard about it. His episodes, or whatever they were, were mostly over by the time Jeremy and Ben met in grad school at UMass, when Jeremy was studying permaculture and Ben had gone back to school for a sustainable engineering degree. The two became close despite the 30-year difference in their ages. They were mentor and student, almost father and son. Since Ben and I don't have children, we have—had—a habit of fondly collecting stray young adults. When Ben's parents decided to create a cooperative living arrangement, we gathered our friends and our strays and formed a family. Having Jeremy and Zoe join us made perfect sense and the co-op worked beautifully. Until it didn't.

That was my husband's fault. And mine.

It *could* have been okay. The grid take-down that Ben and his anarchist buddies planned and carried out so well *might* have had a happy outcome, *might* have opened blindfolded eyes to the climate emergency and goosed people into action. We *might* have all lived happily ever after.

But none of those things came to pass.

Instead, when the electrical grid went down for about a quarter of the country, Virginia to Maine and west almost to Chicago, it left millions of people with no heat or power or Internet for eight days in November. Our co-op took in as many neighbors as we could, but of course that was nothing compared to the numbers affected; city and state emergency services were stretched way beyond capacity, leading to curfews, shelter-in-place orders, and general social chaos. There was collateral damage. People died, mostly the elderly and vulnerable.

Ben was arrested on the eighth night of Chanukah, just weeks after the grid failure, and charged under a federal terrorism statute. That was more than our co-op could handle. One family left immediately, claiming pacifism as their reason. This left an empty apartment for Zoe's dad Sam, and Patty, and we were happy to have their company and support. A year later, after failed negotiations complicated by the pandemic, Ben and his co-conspirators accepted a plea bargain. The accusations and attacks continued and grew, both external and internal. People shunned us at the grocery store; they wrote condemning letters to the editor of the local newspaper, and ugly emails. The internal strife was even worse, our arguments ranging from tactical political disagreement to deep philosophical differences. Was Ben a hero or a terrorist? A martyr or a dupe? Brilliant or misguided? The disagreements spiraled downward into fierce fights about how to hang the toilet paper in the common bathrooms. More collateral damage, trivial edition.

We tried hard to repair the rift, but the pandemic hit just weeks after Ben's arrest, intensifying every emotion. The passionate camaraderie of our cooperative became thin and brittle, and then it snapped. We were isolated and frightened, both of Covid and of the FBI still nosing around, worried there could be more arrests. Another family considered leaving, since their twins' daycare was closed indefinitely, but instead the babies' grandparents moved into the guest apartment to help with childcare.

No matter how we tried to adapt and compromise and be kind to each other over the next months, tensions festered and grew.

The final blow, the one that finished us off, was when Ben's father, who insisted on working too many shifts at the local emergency room even though he was retired, succumbed to the virus. Miriam is still numb with the loss, barely speaking. Late one winter night, as she and I huddled in front of the wood stove in the family room, she admitted being torn in two. "I adore my son, but can't help blaming Ben for his father's death," she whispered. "Even though Covid killed my love, it was Ben's actions that broke him."

I live in a similar limbo of love and blame, support and anger. Ben is my lover and best friend. In my mind, he's a living avatar of Dr. Seuss, the Lorax and the Sneetches rolled into one tall, skinny, cowlicked, goofy-grinned character. Ben's actions with the grid came from the purest place I know; how could it have gone so wrong? And how can my heart hold such contradictory emotions about him? How can I want to simultaneously pummel his chest with my fists in fury and unbutton his shirt, trailing kisses down his body?

Our co-op teetered as well, from love and sadness to anger and blame. Our decade-long experiment with urban off-the-grid communal living, sharing our money and our lives, and trying to build a new kind of family was failing. We had no plans for dissolving our connection because we never dreamed it would end.

Ben's activism, as misguided as some of us thought it might have been, did open our eyes. The climate emergency was here. It was inevitable and it would be increasingly brutal. Some of us talked about wanting to live somewhere north and inland, someplace that would be less devastated by the climate crisis, at least in the short term. A place where we could rebuild the co-op and figure out how to make things a little better for ourselves and our community in the interim. We had no illusions about the government—any government —making the major systemic changes needed to turn the disasters away.

Amid all these competing and conflicting emotions, we endured a series of bitter and heartbreaking co-op meetings. At our last meeting, Miriam, who had somehow functioned as the co-op chairperson through all this turmoil, stood silently in front of the wood stove until we all quieted. She had dressed up for the occasion, wearing the jewel-tone quilted jacket she had worn to her wedding so many decades before. She held a slim volume of poetry, opened it to a well-worn page.

"The Death of the Small Commune," she said. "Written sixty

years ago by Marge Piercy." When she got to the part about turning over earth and planting seeds and thinning the green shoots, I looked at Jeremy, understanding a bit more.

We all sobbed as she read, for once in emotional connection with each other. Then Miriam presented us with a framed hand-lettered broadside of Piercy's words, illustrated by her own colorful crane paintings, before resigning as the co-op chairperson.

We were on the verge of splitting into two groups. Myesha, in her adolescent manner of ridiculing everything the older co-op members said or did, dubbed us the Leavers and the Stayputs. The meeting to make the final decision was scheduled for this evening.

All these thoughts wrestled in my mind as I stared at Jeremy curled up in hay and chicken shit. Jeremy's mishigas with the body-invaders and voices couldn't have come at a worse time.

## Jeremy

Jeremy sighed deeply and stood. He brushed the hay off his jeans, scraped chicken poop from his boots, and picked up the basket of eggs. He leaned over and patted the Rhode Island Red. "Thanks for the company," he whispered, then turned to face Sarah.

"Are you okay now?" Sarah asked.

He shrugged. "Don't know. Guess I need to find Patty."

"She's in the kitchen, waiting for the eggs."

Jeremy handed Sarah the basket. "I'll be down in a few minutes."

He watched her amble through the rooftop gardens, surprised at the gray strands in her dark hair. She paused to pick a shiny September basil leaf and stick it in her mouth before disappearing down the stairs. He knew he should follow her, talk to Patty, try to understand what just happened. When they completed his informal therapy years before, they had concluded that his plant hallucinations might be a gift rather than a disease. So maybe he should welcome his gift back into his life, at a time when he could certainly use some guidance from the universe.

He should get downstairs. There was work to do. He should try to help Sarah, who had reluctantly inherited/accepted the co-op chair position and needed all the support they could offer. Every time they discussed closing their co-op bank account or dividing up the volumes on the family room floor-to-ceiling bookshelves, she choked up and left the room. Thinking of her, he started toward the stairs.

Walking along the garden pathway, he felt a surge of pride mixed with sorrow. When he and Zoe joined the co-op, he thought the idea of growing plants and raising chickens on a roof was nuts. Why couldn't they buy land and farm like normal people? But there was no farmland available near their repurposed factory building, and the football field-sized rooftop expanse was intriguing. Once Ben explained that the space under the solar array would offer shade to complement the sunny parts, it clicked in his mind. They could do this, he had thought. And they had.

He was pleased by how easily the other co-op members embraced permaculture theory and techniques, how eagerly they helped with the planting and harvesting. If he and Zoe joined the Leavers, it would be crazy-hard to leave this behind. Even if he took seeds and small plants with him, even with the excitement of planning a new garden, it would feel like losing a limb. That thought made him look at his hands, remember the vines growing from them just a few minutes ago, the creepers wrapped around his arms and legs. He rubbed his hands over the sleeves of his flannel shirt and flicked a feather off his elbow.

If he and Zoe left this place, what would that mean for her desire to start a family? Would he feel less terrified at the prospect elsewhere? Hard to imagine that could be so, in a new place, with a newly reconfigured family. The last time he and Zoe talked about it, about staying versus going, she asked him a surprising question. "Why do you feel so responsible for everything and everyone?" she asked. He didn't know.

So many unanswered questions. Why were the vines back? What were they trying to tell him, with such urgency that they used language? Last time, their message was about the loss of plant species, and that hadn't gotten any less catastrophic, so there must be something new. Something especially urgent. Was it related to their current situation? He'd read the research about plants making audible sounds, at frequencies higher than humans can hear, when they were stressed. Did the plants have something to say about Ben's actions? How did vegetables feel about terrorism?

## Sarah

As we gathered in the co-op family room that evening, I took some deep breaths and tried to read the mood of the group by who sat where. It wasn't difficult. Albie and Rachel and Myesha had pulled their chairs close to Miriam and me on the sofa. Jeremy squeezed in next to us on the other end and Zoe parked her wheelchair next to him. Zoe's dad Sam and Patty sat on the loveseat. On the other side of the wood stove sat the rest of the group.

I sat there, mute. I simply didn't know how to begin this conversation. Rachel came to my rescue, which is one of the reasons why she's my BFF. She cut right to the chase, which is another reason.

"Does anyone feel this co-op has a chance of surviving our disagreements?" she asked. "Of moving forward together?"

No one spoke. We had exhausted this conversation in the past few weeks.

"Okay," I said into the silence. "How do we go about dissolving this family?"

There were so many details to work out, from the finances to the timing. The Stayputs, with the help of their new members, would remortgage the building and buy us out, so we would have funds to start over, somewhere new. We argued about when to leave, how to divide our food and solar panels, how to end one life and begin another. Somehow, by the end of the meeting, we settled on a compromise: Ben's solar panels and batteries would stay, but the food and whatever plants we could carry would go.

Go where? We didn't have a clue. We had strong western Massachusetts roots, and the thought of leaving our renovated factory building with its view of Mt. Tom was devastating. The meeting ended late, after midnight, but we were slow to disperse. I sat rooted to my spot on the sofa, unable to move. I felt both relieved that it was done, decided, but also terribly sad. Emptied out. I also felt strangely disappointed in all of us, that we hadn't been able to negotiate a truce, to be kind enough to each other's ways of looking at the world to figure out how to continue to live together. Ben would have patched together a compromise, I thought, but then remembered that his passion had landed us in this impossible situation.

I admit I wasn't paying much attention to the other people in the room, though I was vaguely aware that people were milling about and gathering tea mugs and sweaters on their way upstairs to their own apartments. I wasn't thinking about Jeremy, still sitting next to me on the sofa, until I heard a soft murmuring. *Feet in earth*, it sounded like, or *Feet deep in earth*. But it wasn't his voice.

Honestly, I'm not sure if I saw this, or imagined it in my sorrowful state. The singsong words appeared to float from mint green vines that sprouted out of his fingers, coiled around his arms like living springs, reached toward his shoulders and neck. I flinched as a thin filament burrowed into the soft flesh above his clavicle. That must hurt!

Had the plants escalated their tactics, so that others could see them? Or was I so unhappy and undefended that I could share Jeremy's hallucination?

"Are you okay?" I asked, leaning toward him, but I don't think he heard me. His lips moved in time to the plant-songs: *Feet in earth. Plant deep in earth. Every foot in earth.* Something like that.

"Zoe!" I called out. She left the dishes she was stacking in the sink and wheeled over. I guess she had seen him like this before, in this plant invasion. Except that it didn't appear to be an invasion because somehow Jeremy welcomed the vines. More of a visit. In any case, Zoe nodded at me and arranged the temperature-blanket she knit him for Chanukah around Jeremy's shoulders, taking care not to injure the vines, real or not. Together, we helped him stand, shrouded in the striped blanket of climate doom, and walked him toward the elevator. He didn't protest, didn't stop singing with the leaves, just chanted tenderly and walked with Zoe, using her wheelchair for balance.

I must have imagined that impossible stalk of spiky green vegetable matter trailing behind him along the floor.

## Ellen Meeropol

### Jeremy

He woke up clear-headed the next morning but refused to open his eyes. He remembered the vines visiting and that he had been able to understand their words much better this time. *Feet in earth. Plant each foot in earth.* Not that he fully understood what it meant. But that would come. He didn't want to get up and face the day. Didn't want to start making plans to leave his home. Didn't want to contemplate what additional tasks faced him in following the message from the plants.

Zoe touched his arm. "Patty's here. Put your robe on and come talk to her."

He shook his head.

"Yes," Zoe said. "Now. Please."

She left the room, letting the smell of fresh coffee in before closing the door again. He smiled, thinking about the coffee wars, back when how much money to spend on free-trade, fresh roasted beans was their biggest co-op battle. Miriam still wept when she smelled the aroma her husband had loved most in the world. She claimed it was the worst part of widowhood, not being able to enjoy a cappuccino without that fist squeezing her heart.

The door opened again, this time for Patty carrying two cups. She put them on his bedside table and pulled a chair closer to the bed.

"Do you want to talk about it?" she asked.

He took a long drink of the coffee.

She waited.

He wondered how patient she could be, but then chided himself for being stubborn or childish. Or something.

"They've come twice," he finally said. "Yesterday morning and again last night. They're speaking this time."

She nodded.

"And they're escalating. I think Sarah saw them this time. That's new."

Patty sipped her coffee.

"They're telling me something about planting feet in the earth."

"What does that mean to you?" she asked. "Is it a metaphor?"

He laughed. "No, I think they want us to actually plant ourselves. In the earth. Try being vegetables for a change."

## Sometimes an Island

Patty tilted her head to the side. He remembered that gesture. He always thought it meant that he had said something interesting or smart. Or maybe silly.

"How do you picture that, Jeremy? Being vegetables for a while?"

"Maybe humans should have to spend two years as a plant, kind of like compulsory military service, to understand what we're doing to our planet."

Patty smiled. "How would that work?"

"How the fuck do I know how it would work? It's not my idea. But I admit I like it. Maybe then people would get how badly we've ruined the soil, poisoned the water, disrupted the natural cycles. They'd feel it themselves, in their bodies."

"Then what?"

He shook his head. "No idea. Look, I know it's crazy, but I think that's the message from the vines: *plant feet in earth.*" He shrugged and finished his coffee.

Patty stood up. "Let's talk more later, okay?"

"Whatever," Jeremy said. "We have a Leavers meeting this morning, don't we?"

"At ten. But you must deal with this issue too, Jeremy."

He shook his head again, harder. "No. It's not an issue. It's a message, an important one, and I'm paying attention." He looked at her. "Are you?"

### Sarah

I admit to being terrified as the other Leavers straggled into our—no, *my*—apartment. I had dragged Ben's desk into the bedroom to make more room in the small living room. We'd never had to have meetings in apartments before but using the co-op family space downstairs no longer felt appropriate. With our four kitchen chairs, the sofa, Ben's recliner, and Zoe's wheelchair, we gathered in a snug circle.

There were nine of us, ranging in age from Myesha at 16 to Miriam at 76. Where should we go? What could we do?

I looked around the group. How would we support ourselves in a new place? In terms of skills and professions, our group was in good shape regarding healthcare, with a nurse practitioner and an RN, but we were light on the skills necessary to survive without the infrastructure of society. Ben had been the one who designed and kept our solar panels and batteries working, with Albie's help. Albie was a mechanical genius with PTSD courtesy of his military service, though he'd been known to respond with violence at the term *service*. Sam was a web designer and a hacker, but we couldn't count on the stability of the Internet. Rachel was trained as an engineer. Even though she had never worked with solar voltaic arrays, she'd been working with Albie and studying Ben's extensive library. Maybe, between Albie and Rachel, we could survive off the grid. With Jeremy's permaculture knowledge, my work combating food insecurity, and all of us helping with gardening and canning and raising chickens, we could feed ourselves. We hoped.

We sat in our circle, silent, all looking out the wall-sized triple glazed window, easily both the biggest expense in designing our apartments and the most glorious aspect of them. The late morning sun ignited the trees on top of Mt. Tom, alive with the beginnings of autumn's colors. The question of what next felt bigger than any mountain, more impossible than any challenge we had faced so far.

The answer to *Where* came from one of our youngest members.

Zoe's people came from an island off the coast of Maine. Last winter she went there for a relative's funeral and connected with some cousins. She fell in love with the place, kept talking about how much she wanted to live there. With rising sea levels, Jeremy convinced her an island wasn't a great idea. But Zoe had stayed in touch with two cousins on her mother's side, Laura and Sadie. Sadie and her husband called themselves climate refugees and had bought a parcel of land in Somerset County, Maine. Their son and his Brooklyn family had already joined them, and others were considering it. They were trying to build an intentional community, a different sort of co-op. It would be off-the-grid, self-supporting, and the center of interconnected farms and cottage industries, building a network of people living in harmony, powered by the sun and the wind.

"A great opportunity. Right?" Zoe asked. "And we're invited." She turned to Jeremy. "They could really use your permaculture experience. You'll have lots of people to help. Of course, it's very rural," she added. "Crappy cell service, no broadband Internet."

"No way!" Myesha stood up. "I can't live without Internet."

Jeremy nodded. "It's hard. I've read that when people have to give up the web, and GPS, and all that, at first it's like they've lost limbs, lost senses. Then they learn how to see again, how to make things. It's better, after a while." His words trailed off, sounding uncertain.

"Maybe that's true," Patty said. "But if any of us are hoping to work remotely, to help support the group, the lack of Internet access would make it impossible."

"You know we can't *count* on the grid," Jeremy said, trying to keep the edge of annoyance from his voice. "Didn't you learn anything from Ben? The grid will fail. We're on our own, people."

"Which is why we need a community, working together." Zoe touched his hand.

Jeremy rubbed his eyes. "I like the idea, but are these people, your relatives, serious about building a new culture? It'll take more than a cow-fart tax or growing our own food. If people are going to survive what's coming—the cascading fires and drought and storms..."

"Sounds pretty Biblical," Sam offered. Trying to lighten us up, I suspect.

Jeremy wouldn't have it. "It's *science*. We can expect multiple crises, building on each other. Ben taught us this."

"Maybe we should leave Ben out of this," Sam said.

"No, Ben is part of all of it, even if he's in prison," Jeremy insisted. "He taught us that people need to live in smaller groups, with much less stuff. And that we need to drastically rethink how we view our human history, turn what we used to think 180 degrees around. Instead of teaching kids how wonderful all those inventions were, like the steam engine and chemical fertilizers and burning fossil fuels, we need to teach about unintended consequences for the planets and its species. Collateral damage."

"What about your vines?" Patty asked.

"They're on our side." Jeremy smiled. "And I think we're doing what they want."

The group was quiet.

"You don't change the world by running away," Albie said. "Running backwards. Back to the land movements didn't work out so well the first time."

"And Ben's radical activism didn't work out so well, did it?" Sam said. "He—"

"This is different," I interrupted. "This isn't just to save ourselves. It's to re-imagine how people could live together in community without destroying the planet."

"The human race has already accomplished much of the destruction," Jeremy said. "This is, we hope, beginning a remedy."

"In any case, I'm not so sure about Maine," Rachel said, quietly.

"It's close to Ben's prison," I said. "Easier to visit him."

"Yeah, but it's awfully white."

"Maybe it's not always about race, Babe." Albie patted Rachel's hand.

"Everything's about race, Papa," Myesha countered.

Zoe nodded. "That's true, especially rural Maine. But my cousin Laura is thinking seriously about moving to the farm. Her kid is Black. And you guys, and Jeremy."

"And if the neighbors are racist?" Rachel asked.

"Then we'll deal. They could be anti-Semitic too," Miriam spoke up for the first time. "You're Black. I'm a Jew. Neither of us is safe in the world, never will be. A fact of life."

"Maybe a fact of death," Rachel muttered.

Despite worries about the short growing season and unfamiliar crops, despite anticipating unpredictable weather with droughts and floods and fire, despite not knowing Zoe's people, despite fears about being too different demographically from our new community, we decided to go to Maine.

"I hope this works," Miriam said.

"Let's hear it for the nine musketeers!" Sam proposed.

Zoe patted her belly. "Make that ten."

# Perish the Thought
## the island · 2024 · Tillie, Esther

### Tillie

This afternoon my family went to swim in the quarry on the other side of the island. Mom asked one of us to stay home with you, my Esther, my alte bubbe, my great-grandmother, and I volunteered right away. Partly because you're wicked old and who knows if you'll still be alive when we visit next year. Partly because I like this ancient house, all uneven floors and creaky stairs. When I was little, I loved that the kitchen sink was set low so I could reach the faucet. People were shorter back then, you told me.

You don't talk much these days, so it's not always easy hanging out with you, to know what you're thinking. Sometimes you get spacy and don't answer. Like right now—do you even know I'm here? Mom says you've become a little forgetful so I remind myself to be patient. So I'm quiet too, thinking my own thoughts and watching memories flicker across your face.

When we finish our tuna sandwiches, I put the dishes in the child-sized sink.

"Want some tea?" I ask.

You nod slightly, not that enthusiastic. Making tea is something to do and then I have things I want to ask you. I fill the kettle. It's cool that you grow the spearmint plants in your jumbled garden out back, then hang them upside down in the kitchen to dry the leaves, which go into a silly metal contraption with holes, instead of the real way with tea bags.

"Let's sit on the porch," I say, walking with you to the side-by-side rocking chairs. I go back for the tea and set our mugs on the wobbly table. We both look down the rocky slope, overgrown with blueberry bushes and beach plums, to the bay. You do that thing where you go all quiet and stare off into some place I can't see.

I've been coming to this island pretty much every summer since I was born. Mostly, I love it, except for too many relatives—aunts and uncles and cousins twice removed—and I can't keep everyone straight. All the boring old people—not you—tell me how much I've grown. Last year I spent a lot of time rolling my eyes and escaping down the path to the pebble beach that kills my bare feet, but I'm sixteen now.

This summer is different. It's our first time back to the island since my parents dragged my sisters and me to live in the *other* Maine, the inland part with mountains and moose instead of ocean and relatives. I don't much like it there and I bet you wouldn't either, Esther. I see how you look at the wild island coast. You're the one who showed me the sparkles on the wavelets in the late afternoon sunlight. An army of Tinkerbells, you called them. You taught me how to tell an osprey from an eagle. You explained how the color of the bay changes with time of day and weather and clouds and light. But now the seas are rising and there are wildfires everywhere, even in Brooklyn, so my family had to move and live all squished in with my grandparents in the middle of nowhere. After a year, when I was just starting to get used to it, a bunch of people, cousins and their friends, from Massachusetts joined us. They're building a new wing on the house while we're here this summer. I'm glad to be here, to tell you the total fucking truth.

I glance at you quickly, worried that I might have said that out loud and you don't like bad language, but you don't react so I must have just thought it.

I don't love living in that inland Maine and I miss J, my bae back in Brooklyn who hardly ever texts anymore. But there's one good thing at my new high school. This climate group I started with two other girls has grown into a Big Thing. Actually, it's gotten a bit out of hand and I'm not sure what we should do when school starts again in a couple of weeks. I'm stressed out about it, actually. I've tried

*Sometimes an Island*

texting J, but they don't answer, only care about their own stuff these days.

You murmur something and shiver. I help you into your favorite gray cardigan, hanging on the back of your chair, even though it's August and warm. I stroke your arm because I get that life has been hard for you, too. You and Rufe were married forever. I can't imagine loving someone all those years and then they die and leave you. I whisper the names you call him.

"Bashert," which is Yiddish for soulmate. And then "habibi," which I don't exactly know what it means but your voice goes all liquid when you say it. You told me that without him, without your bashert-habibi, you're bereft. That's a sorrowful word but I like how it feels on my tongue. Be-reft.

We've always shared a love of words. But talking isn't so easy this year. For one thing, I don't know if you would approve of J and me, so I don't talk about them with you. Not that it matters any more since they're ghosting me. Ghosted or not, I'm bereft without J. My bae. My bashert-habibi-bae.

You take a sip of tea, make a face like it tastes ugly, and put the mug down. Your eyes go all soft and unfocused, like you see something in your mind's eye, something that's not actually here.

After a minute, you start talking in a different voice, with an accent like you're back in Russia instead of on this rocky island in Penobscot Bay. Like you've grown backwards and you're not old anymore. It's hard to follow but I think you're telling me about sneaking out of a village late at night to come to America. About how the Cossacks hate Jews and kill us in pogroms and you have to escape. You tell it like it's happening right now, right here, even though we're on this boring, safe island.

It makes me shiver even though it's warm.

"Wait a minute," I interrupt you. "I thought it was the Nazis who killed Jews."

You come back to now for a moment. "Hitler didn't invent hate, Tillie," you say. "He just perfected it."

We both stare down the yard toward the jumble of stones and seaweed at the water's edge and across the Sound. I wonder what you see over there, other than scrub pines and the wake trailing a fishing boat. Your eyes go fuzzy again and it's almost like you become another person, a different person who's hiding inside you. You sit up straighter and hold your shoulders back. When you speak, your voice sounds young. Scared.

"The men came last night, men on horses," you whisper. "They carried axes and blazing torches. They yelled nasty curses and smashed all the windows, then set the houses on fire. My big sisters and I covered our noses with our shawls for the smoke and hid in the barn until dawn, burrowed under the hay with the scurrying mice, so the bad men couldn't find us and hurt us like they did Mama."

I want to ask what the men did to your mama, but I don't want to hear the answer. I can guess.

"Could this happen again?" I ask instead. "Cossacks and Hitler?"

"Perish the thought," you mutter before disappearing back into the past.

I look at you, wondering if you're losing it, but you seem so sane. So smart.

Okay, this is getting spooky. I've read all those time-travel novels, but who wants to live in one?

### Esther

You must think I'm gaga, Tillie. Maybe I am. Half the time I'm me, 84 years old and on that slow slide to the long night where I hope, but don't really expect, to be reunited with my Rufe. Or his ghost. Or whatever.

But more and more often these days, I become Deborah, my own grandmother. Don't ask me how it happens because I can't explain it to you. Something shifts in my head and my eyesight ignites like spiraling stars, then I slip into Deborah's skin, into her long skirt that hangs to her ankles. I tie her apron strings behind my back. I wind her dark brown braids around my head. I *become* Deborah mother of Elizabeth who is mother of me, Esther, who is mother of Sadie who is mother of Marc who married Evelyn who is mother of Tillie. Of you, a smart girl who can't make a decent cup of tea and probably wishes you were anywhere on the planet but here on this porch with me.

To you and your sisters, this island is vacation land. Every summer your parents schlep you here to this old house. From Brooklyn, where your father went away to college and met your mother and stayed, snapping the thread of island generations, and now moved again to the other Maine. Not unlike my own grandparents, who left their families in the shtetl and moved to this rocky island and stayed here and grew new families and became part of this place. We are a people who are eternally hated and attacked and forced to move. We try our best to put down roots in foreign soil full of stones.

Before Rufe got sick, I never traveled back to Deborah's world. The first time it happened, I was sitting in our living room next to his rented hospital bed. Rufe insisted they transfer him back home from the hospital in Bangor so he could die on his island, looking through the spray-fogged window to the Sound and beyond, to whatever comes next. Becoming Deborah that first time happened suddenly, violently, without warning. Maybe it happened because Rufe was so close to death and that let Deborah get close. That sounds crazy, doesn't it? Anyway, it shook me badly, but Rufe was too sick to notice and I never told anyone. Not even Mary, who might have believed me.

Part of my brain knows I'm here, today, sitting with you, Tillie. But some impossibly true part of me is back in 1903. And I want you to know this truth, so I try to explain.

"I'm my grandmother," I tell you. My body shudders with something like memory but more intense because it's happening right now. "I'm Deborah and it's the worst day of my life. I'm ten years old, the baby of the family. The pogroms in our village near Odessa have gotten bloodier. After the bad men set fire to our house, my older sisters and I run to the barn. We cover our ears to muffle our mother's cries. The rains come then, and the men go quiet and we hope they're gone. We shiver all night, trying not to weep, because sobbing might attract attention. I'm wearing our mother's favorite orange scarf, which I stuff into my mouth to muffle myself."

You look at me like I'm nuts.

I won't give up. I can't stop the telling. "Shortly before dawn, my papa comes from the forest to take us away. My sisters refuse to leave our home. They are women, with minds of their own, but I'm still a child. Our father tells me to pack one satchel with my most precious things while he and his two friends load the cart with food and blankets. I dig through the smoking embers of our half-burned home and find the metal box where I keep my treasures. I pack the nesting dolls and my two beloved books and the necklace with a Jewish star my mother gave me but told me not to wear until it's safe."

I want you to understand, Tillie, but you shake your head.

"You've lost me," you say. "What are you talking about?"

"I'm talking about what happened to our people," I say. "In the Pale of Settlement. Before we came to the island."

"I know that Rufe's father and your father were best friends in Russia," you say. "And they moved here with Aunt Anna's grandfather forever ago. But no one told me *why* they left. Why didn't anyone tell me this?"

"Who wants to talk about such horrible things?"

"What does that mean, the Pale of Settlement?" you ask. "That's where our nesting dolls came from, right?"

A fist of memory squeezes my heart, fierce with whispered stories and imagined sepia photos of those who perished. I have no breath and can't speak, not even to you, my sweet Tillie. Instead, I'm back in Deborah's skin, in the bedroom I share with my sisters. I hide the Star of David in the second to smallest nesting doll for safekeeping and then wrap the matryoshkas in my favorite nightgown for protection. My father yells at me to hurry so I add a few smoke-stinky clothes to the satchel and join him. As the sun rises, my father and I leave the only home I've ever known.

The knees of my papa's trousers are dirty, and his hands too, and I realize he has just buried my mother.

## Tillie

"The Pale of Settlement?" I ask again. "What's that?"

You look pale and your voice is tired when you answer. "The only place Jews were allowed to live. Parts of Russia and Poland and Ukraine. Some other countries too because the borders kept changing. It's the place we're from. The place we had to flee. Decades before the Holocaust. Don't they teach you anything in school?"

I ignore that. "And the dolls? That's where you got the nesting dolls on the mantel?"

"Deborah carried the matryoshka dolls when she left. She

brought them to Maine and gave them to me on my sixteenth birthday. I gave them to your cousin Emma on her sixteenth birthday, but she asked Sadie to hold them for her, to take them with her to the homestead inland. For safekeeping."

Those nesting dolls are like the family jewels or something. Always displayed on one mantel or another, but they're not for playing.

"I'm sixteen." I try not to whine. "Why didn't I get them?"

You shrug. I get it, since Emma lives with you and you two are close.

I could ask Sadie about it, but it's probably a bad idea. Sadie is annoyed with me. That makes me sad because even if she drives me bonkers now that we live in her house, she *gets* me. She's the person who gave me my clay doggie, and she goaded me to start a climate catastrophe group since there wasn't one at the high school. I don't think she believes the catastrophe part, but whatever. Then everything went crazy last year, after the fossil fuel protests and the National Guard shootings and then the Gaza war and all the hate crimes. Sadie got scared. She started advising caution, backing away from her support, and I called her a coward so she's not my biggest fan right now.

Our school group was split too, in thirds, between peaceful protests at town hall, civil disobedience at Big Samson's Oil and Gas, and slashing the tires of every SUV and pickup we could find. We disagreed and argued and couldn't decide anything. We put off the decision until school starts in September and agreed to reach out over summer vacation to other high school climate activists.

That's how I met Annie, trying to save the planet. She's got red hair and freckles and loves to paint and she's really good at it. She goes to a prep school a couple of hours from Portland and works part time at a horse farm. She started a climate group at her school too, and every week when my family went to the town library, we talked on FaceTime. At first it was all about climate stuff, trying to figure out how to convince the old people they had to stop using fossil fuels so their grandchildren would have a future, but then it was about everything. I've called her a couple of times from the island this month, using my cousin's computer. Personally, I'm leaning toward the tire-slashing option and so is Annie. We agree about a lot of things.

Sadie has been trying to change my mind all summer.

I wonder what *you* think we should do, Esther. You're smart and I trust you. But you look like you're sleeping in your chair now, pale and exhausted. You look... depleted.

"Are you okay, Esther?" I whisper and take your hand.

You squeeze my hand, silent.

*What would Deborah think?* I wonder. She understood imminent danger—watching people around her perishing, needing to do something drastic to survive. What would she advise about tactics? Should we be careful because the world can be harsh and ugly and everything can change in a minute? Or risk arrest but be peaceful? Is that too cautious, too chicken? Should we be daring and break the rules and give everything we have, even our lives, to try to change the world?

But then, how could Deborah know, all those years ago? You can't flee climate disaster, like our family did with the Cossacks.

## Esther

I was heartbroken when my girl Sadie and her David left for their mainland homestead and I miss them terribly, but not enough to go live in some other place that isn't home. I've lived in this old house my whole life. I was born and grew up here, went to the island school, birthed my children and raised them in this old house. Rufe is buried here and I will join him.

Can you understand that, Tillie? I want to ask you, but it's too much work to open my eyes and talk.

My life these past few years hasn't been much of a picnic. Rufe's illness and death was the worst part, and losing Mary was almost as hard. She and I were cousins and best friends since we were toddlers. And every week now there's news that this old friend had a stroke, or a second cousin's no-big-deal cancer metastasized to his brain, or a neighbor down the road was just diagnosed with Parkinson's.

You're so young, my zissele. To the young, life stretches ahead of you forever. You think you've discovered things no other generation could understand. Like you and your friend J. You think you're the

## Sometimes an Island

only girls who love that way? Oh, Tillie, dear Tillie. Listening to you reminds me how full of promise and possibility life can be.

But me, I'm old, and I've lost my Rufe, so why wouldn't I want to live in the past, even a past I never lived in, even an ugly past, if I could have him there?

I can't pretend I'm always in control of slipping into Deborah's life. Usually it just happens; the world sparkles and swirls and spirals and I'm swept away. But sometimes when I imagine her as a young person and try to picture myself in her life, I can send myself back to then. So I take another sip of the too-weak tea, cooled enough to not burn my tongue, and do just that. I picture myself as Deborah at twenty, living right here in this stone house and about to give birth to my mother.

And then I *am* her. My belly is huge, but the rest of me is skinny and strong from working on the farm. My labor is long and hard and I feel myself tear, but Elizabeth is perfect. She has the Saperstein eyes, hazel with golden speckles like my mother. I've never been so happy and so forlorn. I weep because my mother will never in this life meet her granddaughter. Does that make sense to you, Tillie? I weep for me too, because I don't know the first thing about babies. My cousins will help, but it's not the same as a mother.

You lean over and wipe my cheek. "Why are you crying, Esther? What's wrong?"

I shake my head. I won't share this moment with you. You already think I'm demented. "Just a bit of a headache, sweetheart," I lie. "I think I'll take a nap."


### Tillie

It's not a headache. I see the way you sit up straight and how your hands stop shaking when you go back there, somewhere, wherever or whenever, to the land of Cossacks and pogroms and burning houses and hiding in barns. And escaping.

I walk with you to the bedroom so you don't fall and break something. I tuck you in with the quilt you made when you were fifteen. I try to imagine making a quilt, but I don't have the time. There's a planet to save.

I'm disappointed. I had hoped to ask you about my problem, about the decision looming ahead about tactics. I have no idea how long you'll sleep and if there will be any time to talk more. I close your bedroom door softly and return to the porch, looking out at the Sound and the haunted little island beyond, a magnet for drama and heartbreak for centuries.

I breathe deeply and the fresh, soapy smell of your laundry hanging on the line, mixing with the tang of low tide, triggers something in my body. A buzzing around the edges of my vision, a tingling in my skin, an electricity in my fingers, like the shock when you touch the short in the faucet of the outdoor shower that no electrician has ever been able to fix. The sunlight sparkles and the waves shimmer and my vision gets all golden-hued and pearl-edged. The low tide aroma swells and fills my lungs.

It's a bit like the foggy feeling I got last year when we first moved to the homestead. I touch the clay terrier in my pocket but he doesn't make it stop this time. It's too much. I squeeze my eyes closed. I'm both excited and scared shitless.

Then it's quiet and I open my eyes. I'm no longer on the porch.

I'm in a large garden bordered by forest. The glimmering golden light has morphed into ordinary sunshine. I'm kneeling between rows of carrots next to a woman with wild red curls and freckles. I barely recognize my own hands, thinner and nails grimy with garden soil, but then I see the clay terrier peeking out of a hand-sewn cloth pouch hanging on a leather thong, nestled between my breasts.

I touch the terrier and open my mouth to speak. Only a croak comes out.

"What's that?" the woman asks, pausing from pulling up carrots. When she speaks, I know it's Annie, years older than our FaceTime conversations.

I shake my head, to clear it. What's going on? Who *am* I?

Annie smiles, as if she can hear my unspoken question. "Why, you're my sweet Tillie. Unless you'd like to be someone else today."

Then I get it. I understand.

It's the future and I'm there. I'm twenty-three years old. Annie and I live on a cooperative farm in southern Maine, where she worked every summer during high school and college. We rarely talk about what happened the day last November when everything changed, though we often reminisce how our FaceTime flirting grew into secret visits, then both choosing colleges in Portland, and moving to the farm after graduation. We raise food and horses and repurpose old vehicles and abandoned buildings to build wheeled carts and wagons to transport people and goods in this new world trying to be brave.

We work so hard that sometimes—for an hour or two—I can forget what happened last November. But forgetting isn't healthy, our commune has decided, and we've started sharing stories about the before times. The remembering, the bitter stew of regrets and what-ifs, is harder than the physical labor. If I hadn't lied to my family about Annie. If I had returned to live on the homestead like they wanted me to. If I met them in Portland that day for the family's annual city weekend like I was supposed to, instead of telling them I'd come home for Chanukah. If those things happened...

"...Then you would have perished too," Annie reminds me, rubbing small circles on my back. She has always been able to read my mind.

"Maybe they escaped."

"Possibly." Then she adds, always logical and factual, "But not many people near the coast survived the tsunami."

She's probably right, but it's still possible. I can't stop picturing my grandmother Sadie, who stayed back at the homestead that day to hang out with Miriam, whose dementia made travel impossible. They might have survived, right?

"Maybe my family was lucky. Maybe my sisters met someone like you. Maybe they found a group of people to survive with. Like I did." I take her hand and press it to my lips. "When can we go to my family, to the homestead? Anyone who made it through the water-hell would try to get home, wouldn't they?"

"Yes," she says. "Probably. But what if there's nothing, no one, there? Won't that be worse?"

"I need to know. I need to see for myself."

"Maybe it's kinder not to know. People perish but your memory keeps them alive."

"That's bullshit," I say. "I'm going. With you or alone."

She puts her arms around me and I breathe in the aroma of garden sweat and homemade lilac soap. "When we finish the harvest," she says, "just three, four weeks. I'll go with you in November. In time for Thanksgiving. It's time I met your family."

"Promise?"

"Promise."

What she couldn't promise, what I could not speak about, was the island. What happened to the island? Is it under water? Are my people there dead?

Tires crunch on gravel, which is jarring because there are no functional cars anymore, not gasoline or electric, not in the Undone world I share with Annie. Then my vision spins in spirals. My fingers tingle again, gentler this time. The sea-light shimmers and the sea-smell fills my nose, tethering me back to 2024. As time settles back into the now, I realize that hours have passed and our beast of a car is coming up the long driveway, my family returning from the quarry.

I sit on the top porch step hugging my knees, trying to understand what just happened to me and what happened to my family. What *will* happen, I guess. Also, wanting *not* to understand. I touch the bisque terrier, tucked in my breast pocket as always. What is the Undoing and when will it happen? What did the tsunami do to the island? So many questions. My being in the garden with Annie is a ghost-scene, only half-remembered. Did I dream it? Why aren't I more freaked out?

Before the car comes into sight, I slip back into the house, into your bedroom, hoping you're awake. But you're snoring, so I sit on the edge of your bed. I wipe a drop of drool from the corner of your mouth with the edge of my tee shirt and look at your wrinkled face for answers, trying to remember what you said before about perishing. Another word that is weighty in my mouth.

The worst day of her life, Esther/Deborah said. What was my worst day? When my parents made me leave Brooklyn? When people who hate Jews burned down my beloved summer camp? The day of the Undoing, which I now know is coming, even though it hasn't happened yet?

In a few minutes, the car doors will slam and my mother will come looking for us. She'll open the door to your bedroom, see you sleeping, and ask what's up. I'll bring a finger to my lips and say you had a headache.

She'll ask if anything interesting happened this afternoon. No, I'll say, crossing my fingers behind my back like I used to when I told a fib.

That's not true, of course, but I can't begin to explain what is.

The truth is that my head is spinning with the possibility that time isn't laid out in a straight line. Could it be true that if the past holds something important to understand, you can loop back to be part of it? It's a wild thought, bubbe Esther, but I like it. If you can connect with your old self, with Rufe, maybe loss stings less. But I went to the future. What determines if you go back or forward in time? Maybe it's about what you need—to understand what happened or figure out how to change the world.

But why me? My grandma Sadie believes that people carry the trauma of their ancestors in their DNA, so I might have Deborah in my cells too. Her wisdom, maybe? If that's true, what is my DNA trying to tell me?

If the future is wise—which is unlikely, given the evidence—maybe my older self can help me figure out how to act now, how to save the planet. Or does none of it matter because the future has happened and everything came undone?

Wish I knew.

I lean over close and rest my head on your chest, feeling the small rise and fall of your breathing.

# Second Chances
## On Zoom · 2026 · Sarah

When the new woman enters the Zoom room, Patty and I exchange glances. That's not easy to do on Zoom, connecting emotions from square to square, but we've had years to perfect the skill. We've developed half a dozen hand signals to communicate warning or worry or to replace an eye roll. Sometimes, if more than a glance or hand signal is needed, we'll private chat, but what if the technology screws up and someone sees our snarky comments?

Tonight, a quick glance is enough. The new woman seems a bit young for our group, which falls somewhere between a women's support group and group therapy. Her hair is barely streaked with gray but her eyes are old. She doesn't look like she's at the end of her rope, but we've all learned that it's sometimes hard to tell.

I'm responsible for bringing the new woman into the group, so it's my fault if this doesn't work out. I barely know her. We met at a virtual national conference for people working in food equality—food banks and pantries and people's farms and CSAs and distribution centers. Before moving to rural Maine, I ran a food pantry in western Massachusetts. Now I coordinate distribution to food insecure folks in my county. The new woman lives in Colorado, I think. Somewhere in the wild west. We hit it off after a workshop on rural and isolated communities and text chatted during the second half of the conference. At one point she asked me how I kept myself from getting too discouraged, especially after the disastrous election, and I mentioned this group. She seemed so lonely that I ended up inviting her to come to a meeting.

Our group has been going for six years. When my husband Ben was arrested, I begged Patty to start a support group for women facing loss because I desperately needed it. Patty had just moved into my co-op and the health center where she worked as a nurse practitioner agreed to sponsor the group. We switched to Zoom meetings in 2020 and that worked well as some of us moved out of the area. Jess was a volunteer at my food pantry and she joined us after her wife died, bringing her neighbor Gloria, who was struggling to rebuild her life after being homeless. Other members came and went, but the four of us have been solid.

Over the years our monthly conversations have ranged from the exquisite pain/pleasure of prison visits to going back to school later in life, from the death of loved ones to climate disasters and endless wars. After the election, things got more grim and we started meeting twice a month, which was particularly challenging for me. Three years ago, Patty and I moved to very rural Maine, where it's hard to find a decent cell phone signal, much less Internet. But one of the local librarians is a neighbor and she lets us use the Wi-Fi in her office.

Over the years, we have been each other's lifeboats, floating adrift in a turbulent sea of angst and existential worry.

Life is messy. Even without the mess, this is the club no one wants to belong to. Our focus on the permutations and combinations of misery could be a real downer, which is probably why the group has shrunk over the past year to just four of us. Five with this new woman.

"Welcome, everyone," Patty begins. "Especially welcome to our guest."

The new woman waves and unmutes herself. "Hello," she says. "I'm Ruby."

Patty welcomes her with a big smile and begins the check-in that opens each meeting. "Since we have a guest tonight, please introduce yourself and say a few words about yourself so Ruby can begin getting to know us." She turned to me. "Will you begin, Sarah?"

I'm not sure why I felt uncomfortable, shy, more awkward than usual, especially since I've already met Ruby.

"Welcome, Ruby," I say. "We've already met, but I'll pretend we haven't and introduce myself. I'm Sarah. I've been in this group since it started seven years ago. In fact, it started because I was so miserable, so bereft, that I begged Patty to start it." I took a deep breath; this part was never easy and it wasn't something I shared with Ruby in our chats. She didn't tell me anything about her history either.

"I was miserable because my husband was arrested for eco-terrorism. Ben has been in prison for five years and I miss him terribly." My eyes tear up, like they always do, still do, when I speak those words. I mute myself, to signal that I'm done talking.

In their Zoom boxes, the group members each make their thumb and forefingers fingers into a heart shape in front of their chests and smile at me. Funny how the simple gesture, which I used to find trite and sentimental, now feels like love.

I return the heart gesture.

"Thank you, Sarah," Patty says. Memories and emotions bounce silently back and forth between us. Patty and her partner Sam moved into our co-op shortly after Ben was arrested and we were both part of the group who moved to Maine when the co-op broke up after Ben's arrest. But rural off-the-grid didn't work for Patty or Sam, or for several of our other friends, and they left last year. I miss Patty every single day, and this group has become even more precious to me.

Patty smiles at me before turning to Jess.

"I'm Jess. My wife died. Breast cancer. Welcome to the group, Ruby."

Patty laughed. "Maybe you could say a little bit more?"

Jess pushed her glasses up on her nose. "Okay. I live in western Massachusetts, where I taught English at a college. I retired when Gee's cancer came back so I could take care of her, be with her. When she died, I fell apart. Totally annihilated. I started writing a novel about her, about our life, and volunteered at the food pantry, which is how I met Sarah. I'm doing better now emotionally, I guess, but I'm lonely. I love this group. You guys are my family."

That finger-heart again. Sometimes I worry we overdo it, but it always feels true.

Patty turns to Gloria. "You missed our last meeting, Gloria. Everything okay with you?"

Gloria's mouth moves but nothing comes out.

"You're muted," Patty reminds her.

"Sorry." Gloria unmutes herself and makes eye contact with Ruby. "Welcome, Ruby. I was a nurse, until I quit my job to take care of my parents. After they died, there was no money and I lived in my car for a couple of years. A friend helped me get my nursing license reinstated and train as a nurse practitioner, specializing in women's reproductive health. It was a rough time, after Dobbs, but women still needed terminations, so we went underground and kept doing the work until someone ratted on us and our network fell apart. I moved back to Massachusetts to lick my wounds. I've been working part-time at Patty's clinic. That's all I've got."

Finger-hearts all around.

"Thanks, Gloria," Patty says. "Ruby, I'm Patty. I'm a nurse practitioner and I started this group years ago, as a support group for women experiencing a crisis in our lives. As you can see, it has sort of morphed into a women's group, like the consciousness-raising groups of the 1960s women's movement. Before you tell us about yourself, Ruby, let me remind you of the guidelines we talked about on the phone. Confidentiality. Kindness. Active listening. Please tell us about yourself."

"Thanks for inviting me," Ruby says. "Like Sarah said, she and I met at an online conference and hit it off. But I don't know if I belong here. Honestly, I don't seem to belong anywhere. I left home at 16 and never went back. I've had no contact with my family, though I know my mother tried to find me for years. She even hired a private detective and he found me but I convinced him to lie to my mother. I admit I was stubborn and refused to talk to her. The thing is, I left my daughter too, and I can't forgive myself for that, so I just don't think about it. Still, I did okay, floating here and there, working at food banks until the pandemic made it harder, and then the election even harder, with the money drying up for food equality work."

"For my work too," Gloria says. "Things have gotten much worse since the election. Even in Massachusetts."

I nodded. I've opened two satellite food pantries, both totally donation-based since the federal funding disappeared.

"It's terrifying, isn't it?" Jess adds. "Realizing how severely out of sync with the country we are."

"What I want to know is who are we, as a people," Gloria asks, "when our society has fallen apart?"

"Time out, please. Let's get back to Ruby's story," Patty says. "Please continue, Ruby. There's more you'd like to share with us, isn't there?"

Ruby rubs her eyes. "The thing is, I've always told myself that I'll return to the island. Maybe even mend some bridges I've pretty much burned down. And it's so weird because these past two-three years I've been dreaming of my mother. Every frigging night. Like she's haunting me. I've always been able to banish her in the mornings until last month, when I turned 50. Then my dreams got more intense, more disturbing, and they don't fade when I wake up. Dreams—nightmares, really—about my parents and my kid and the island, every night about a huge wave sinking Saperstein Neck and..."

You better believe that Patty and I shared a look at that.

"Saperstein Neck?" I interrupt. "Really?"

Patty throws me a "be careful" sign, her right pointer finger on her chin. I knew she was right, but this was incredible.

"No way. Do you know it?" Ruby looks stunned. Not happy stunned either.

I speak slowly, one eye on Patty, not quite sure how to proceed. "I told you that I live with an off-the-grid extended family in Maine. The folks who own the land and started the homestead are refugees from Saperstein Neck. Sadie and David and their son Marc and his family."

"They're my cousins." Ruby speaks slowly. "I had so many cousins on the island. But only one friend, Anna."

Patty holds up her hand. "Is this okay, Ruby? Are you okay?"

Ruby squeezes her eyes closed.

"Small world," I say. Patty's right finger moves to touch her earlobe. That means warning, and I suspect she's right but I can't help myself. "Your friend Anna's daughter, Zoe, is one of my homestead housemates. She learned about the homestead on the ferry to your island."

"My island," Ruby repeats.

I continue, despite Patty's finger dancing around her earlobe now. "Yeah. Anna isn't crazy about the island either, can't bring herself to return. So she convinced Zoe to go in her place, to attend Mary's funeral."

"Funeral?"

Patty mutes us all. "I'm concerned that this is a lot for Ruby. Are you okay?"

Ruby buries her head in her hands and we're all silent for a few moments. Then she unmutes herself. "No wonder my mom is haunting me."

"I'm so sorry, Ruby. You didn't know she died, did you?"

"No." Ruby swipes at her eyes again. "That detective told me when my dad died a few years ago, but no, I didn't know about my mother." She pauses. "Guess I waited too long to go home."

I think she's maybe done, but we wait and yes, more comes.

"The thing is," she continues, her voice so quiet I have to max the volume, "I still have a daughter out there somewhere, too. Her name is Laura and I haven't seen her since she was three."

Should I tell her that I've met Laura, who came to visit the homestead with her husband and daughter—Ruby has a granddaughter!—and has thought about joining us? I glance at Patty, who leans her chin on her fist. Absolutely not; got it. I won't do that. Not yet anyway.

Finger hearts all around as Ruby mutes herself, signaling that she's finished.

The conversation continues, but I space out, thinking of all the interconnections among the five of us and how Ruby is part of us. Thinking that the points of contact weave outward in a spider web of people and places that is both fragile and necessary. Our connections are made of DNA and happenstance, of spit and steel, of scar tissue and loyalty.

I smile at my friends in their Zoom squares, thinking about how in perilous times, we can choose to either open our hearts wide or close them down. It's our choice.

# First Person Plural
the homestead · 2030 · Sadie, Jess, Gloria

### Sadie

On the afternoon the women arrived, Miriam napped and I rested from the morning's garden work. Our elderly tabby slept splayed across my feet, the vibrations from his dieselpurr the closest anyone got to a massage those days. My lap cradled a wicker basket of dead devices. Before the Undoing, when guests entered the homestead, my husband and I collected all screens—phones and tablets and laptops and chargers. Out here in the boonies, with no Internet and only intermittent cell service, the electronics were of little use. David used to say that they represented a privation rather than an opportunity. Everyone was happier with them out of sight, or that's what he believed.

Some days, Miriam was marginally coherent. She could help with peeling potatoes or sweeping the floor, perhaps provide a bit of conversation. Other times, she sat in the maple rocking chair she had brought from the co-op in Massachusetts, muttering about her son in prison and something about cranes. On her good days, I'd set her up at the long pine table with her watercolors and she would disappear into her memories, painting tiny portraits of the people she, we, had lost. This wasn't a good day. She hadn't said a word since waking up that morning.

Sometimes I thought I'd perish from the silence.

## Ellen Meeropol

After the Undoing, those of us who survived searched to find human connection. Timidly, each bruised with loss, silent with grief. The developed world as far as we could know was flooded and poisoned. Without Internet or electricity, media or mail, households and communities could only imagine life beyond their small borders. The floods kept coming, so people needed higher ground, fertile enough to grow food and rural enough to escape the repeated chemical explosions leaking toxic cocktails into the juiced-up winds.

Occasionally, strangers showed up in our rural Maine community. A friend of a friend, sent by whisper of mouth. Needing a place to plant and harvest and eat and sleep and weep. A new family was the last thing anyone wanted. None of us could imagine loving again. Could you?

That's how it was the early June day Jess and Gloria showed up.

Our twenty-acre homestead was conceived as a utopia-by-necessity. Eight years before the Undoing, my husband and I moved here from our Penobscot Bay island home to escape the disasters everyone knew would come, especially to islands. A year later, our son, daughter-in-law and three grandchildren joined us from Brooklyn. Thirty miles of gravel road from the nearest town, this place was wild inland Maine, land of moose and whitewater, weed-choked ponds and stone-littered gardens, hilly and rocky and isolated. From the wide, wrap-around country porch with the two-person hanging swing and rocking chairs, we looked over gardens and meadows to forest and mountains beyond.

Over those years before everything fell apart, others joined us. Our older daughter Lili came one June with her wife and teenage girls, but in August they returned to southern California, unable to make the transition to living in oldie-times and breaking my heart. Our cousin Zoe brought a group from western Massachusetts, victims of a cooperative that broke apart when one of their leaders went to prison for eco-terrorism. They didn't have an easy time acclimating to our simple rural life either, and most of them moved back to civilization. For Myesha, a teenager, not having Internet was simply unacceptable. She almost got a company to agree to bring fiber optic cables, but it took too long and she gave up. Luckily, they stayed long enough to complete a large addition to the house, set up the off-the-grid solar panels with storage batteries, and teach me the bare basics of helping Jeremy maintain the system. Only six of that group were still with us when the Undoing came: our cousin Zoe and her partner Jeremy and their two young children, plus Miriam and her daughter-in-law Sarah, whose husband was in prison near Portland. With me and David and our son and his wife, there were ten of us living off the grid, with my three young adult granddaughters visiting often. We did pretty well, all things considered.

That life-changing event last November, when the Greenland ice cap cracked and crashed and the tsunami started the cascade of disasters, was the day of our annual fall excursion to Portland. Eight folks squeezed into the old van for the drive, eager to buy supplies, to introduce the baby to the ocean, to hang out with Tillie and Rosie and Eloise, and so Sarah could visit her husband in prison.

I stayed home that day with the animals and Miriam, whose neurofibrillary tangles had begun the unraveling process of dementia.

Everyone remembers what happened to the global coastal cities that day. I don't know for certain that my family perished but must assume they did. In the early hours after the tsunami hit, we had news of the cascading disasters, but then the grid failed and the Internet collapsed. We've been cut off, without information. Is it just our region that has returned to pre-industrial life? The country? The world? We don't know.

Any survivors would have made their way home by now, wouldn't they? Or maybe not. Maybe they're hunkered down somewhere and now, with warmer weather making travel easier, they are heading home. That hope sustains me. And destroys me.

For these seven long months, a Maine winter bitter in so many ways, Miriam and I lived on the farm with two dogs, one cat, four goats, and a dozen chickens for company. Our solar panels worked well, and we carefully stored and hoarded our electricity. Our lives were small. I chopped wood, shoveled snow paths to the barns to take care of the animals and collect eggs. I tried to figure out how we would manage to plant and grow and put away enough food come spring to keep us alive next winter. Many evenings that winter I sat in front of the wood stove, fondled the basket of dead devices, and pondered what it meant to be alive when so much of my life was gone.

Why did I keep that hodgepodge of useless gadgets? I did not believe life would ever return to those days when policing screen time was a major parental worry. Of course, everyone took their phones on that last trip to Portland, eager to connect to the Internet and text friends and family. But the older items comforted me with their obsolete links to my missing loved ones. Tillie's discarded tablet with its cracked screen and case plastered with photos of Greta. Evelyn's e-reader loaded with a lifetime's library of feminist fiction and an equal number of mysteries, all digital, all now gagged and silent. I rested my hand on David's battered laptop and let myself feel bereft for a moment. The basket's contents were oddly soothing, as if dusted with broken bits of my family's chromosomes. It reminded me of the junk drawer in the stone house on the island where David and I had lived most of our married life, filled with outdated items like rotary egg beaters and hand-operated can openers, items I wished I hadn't sold for pennies at the tag sale before we moved inland to the farm.

I was remembering that country kitchen, picturing my twin granddaughters standing on chairs at the kitchen counter, splotched with flour and beating eggs for Sunday pancakes, when the call and response of barks and unfamiliar voices in the yard grabbed my attention.

Visitors were unusual. We had an occasional neighbor with a question or bit of news—the kind of thing that would once have merited a text— or rarely, a wanderer asking for milk or bread. How long had it been since I heard a voice other than Miriam's? The old woman spoke less and less. I nudged Democracy off my feet despite her plaintive meow, placed the basket of dead devices on the floor, and walked to the front window, cranked open a sliver to invite the spring breeze. With a mix of hope and fear, I pulled the denim curtains aside just enough to peek out through the screen. Two gray-haired women wearing backpacks pushed bikes with heavy panniers up our dirt driveway. They were backlit by the afternoon sun, but I was pretty sure I didn't know them.

The taller one pointed at a folded map draped over the handlebars.

I checked that Miriam was dozing in her recliner, propped David's old shotgun within easy reach against the wall, and opened the door. Stepping onto the porch, I tried not to notice the chipping paint. I arranged my face in a combination of welcome and warning. I'd only had one problematic visitor, a middle-aged dude who thought two old women on their own would be easy prey. He won't be back.

"Hi," I called to the visitors. "Can I help you with something?"

They stopped about fifteen feet from the porch steps, still holding their bikes. The taller woman smiled. "Are you Sadie?" she asked.

I didn't recognize her. "Do I know you?"

"I'm Jess, from Northampton. This is Gloria. We're friends of Sarah and Patty, from their support group. Sarah told us about this place, about you all. Is she here?"

"Sarah was in Portland. That day."

"I'm so sorry." Jess was silent for a moment before continuing. "We were hoping to join you."

"If you'll have us," Gloria added.

"I know it's kind of pushy," Jess said. "You don't know us at all." She ran her hands through her short hair, leaving it sticking up like a cartoon character. In another circumstance, I would have smiled.

Gloria continued. "Honestly, we're sort of desperate."

I searched their faces, looking for hidden agendas or submerged malevolence. But my yearning for companionship overwhelmed any caution I might have summoned.

"Come rest yourselves." I gestured to the porch swing and rocking chairs. I noticed Gloria take in the toddler-sized rocker and not ask. "I'll make tea."

Over spearmint tea from the garden, the women described their trip north, weeks of riding bikes or pushing them uphill and sleeping in barns when it was too wet for their tents. Superficial talk, while I tried to picture my family making a similar trek home from Portland, if they survived the water. Then Miriam woke up, the afternoon cooled, and we moved inside.

"Why don't you stay tonight," I offered. "We'll get to know each other." Sure, there was risk, but they were friends of Sarah's and I was so deeply hungry for conversation.

We stowed their dusty bikes in the shed and lugged their backpacks and sleeping bags down the hall to the room that belonged to Jeremy and Zoe and their children. "Sorry," I whispered to the pale blue walls.

I added logs to the wood stove. Miriam held Democracy on her lap and scratched her ears. She looked from Jess to Gloria, trying to place them. Gloria sat next to Miriam, leaning over to stroke the old cat's bony back.

"They're guests, Miriam," I told her again, repeating their names. First names. Since the Undoing, we rarely used surnames on the rare occasions we met new people. Maybe because our last names connected us to our people, our ancestors, and we were so deeply ripped away from our pasts, from who we used to be.

Jess pushed her glasses up on her nose and wandered around the room, looking at the small items of our lives. The posters on the wall, the books on the shelves, the tchotchkes on the mantel. I restrained myself from saying anything when she stared at the memory wall. Like most folks, our family photos were buried on useless devices, but Miriam had painted small head shots of everyone. I wouldn't call it a shrine, not exactly, but it was sacred to me. Jess pointed at the image of a small clay terrier missing part of its tail and one droopy ear.

"Sweet," she said. "I bet there's a story here, right?"

There was a story, but it had to do with my prickly and beloved granddaughter, Tillie, and I was not ready to share it with strangers. Jess must have picked up on my emotion because she moved on to the nesting babushka dolls, lined up in descending size along the pine mantelpiece. *Don't touch them,* I silently commanded. I held my breath while Jess looked a moment longer, then sat down.

"Tell us more about yourselves," I invited.

## Jess

I took a deep breath. It was hard to know how to begin. Most survivors divide time into before the Undoing and afterwards. It's different for me. My lifeline fractured the day my sweetheart died.

"My name is Jess. I used to teach English literature at a women's college in the next town over from your friend Sarah's co-op. I met Sarah in a support group." I hesitated then blurted, "My wife died nine years ago, during the pandemic."

"I'm so sorry." Sadie's face arranged itself into the familiar look of empathy.

"Thank you." I took off my glasses and cleaned them with my

flannel shirt, even though they weren't dirty and my shirt was. Ever since Gee died, I've been lost. I know everyone says that, but it is literally true for me. People who knew us as a couple always thought that I was the strong one. Which was true in some ways, but emotionally she was steadfast, centered in herself. Me, not so much it turns out. I didn't know whether to blame the cancer or the virus for her loss. And I desperately needed something to blame. The docs said it was the combination: treatment for the virulent metastases of the breast cancer knocked out her immune system and then, the virus. You know the drill. By now, most of us know it. I also knew I needed to try to build a new life. And I desperately hoped this would be the place. There weren't any other possibilities. So I leaned forward, trying to summon up my old-life charm.

"After she died, I left my job and started working at a local bookstore. I expected, half-hoped, that working in retail I'd catch the virus too and be put out of my misery. But I didn't, and being around all those books, the ones I'd taught for decades and the new ones, I became a cliché and started writing a novel."

"That's so cool. What's it about?" Sadie asked.

I got that Sadie didn't want to talk about loss. Unfortunately, my manuscript wasn't very cheerful. "About an old woman's rather unfortunate adventure being tortured on a little island in Penobscot Bay."

Sadie looked stunned. "Hurricane Island? I've heard rumors about nasty stuff over there. I lived most of my life on the next island over."

Would this help or hurt us?

"Wow," Gloria said, looking from Sadie to me and back. "That's quite a coincidence."

Just what we needed. A painful reminder of home and possibly a reason for Sadie not to want us here. I wondered what she knew, what she thought, about the secret activities over there. Did she have kin who worked there? I hoped that evil place was under water now.

I must have looked distraught because Sadie touched my shoulder and said again, "I'm sorry for your loss."

"You lost a partner too, right?"

"David," she said. "Missing. They're all missing. One daughter and her family in California. Our son and his family who lived here with us, all five of them. They were in Portland that weekend. Our friends too, who lived here with us.

"Sarah."

Sadie's face crumpled.

I had to change the subject before we had a group weep. We didn't know each other well enough for that.

"I know, I'm laughably predictable," I continued. "Has there ever been an English teacher who didn't imagine herself writing the Great American Novel?" My tone was joking, but writing this novel saved my sanity. I had a first draft finished and was deep into revisions when the outside world fell apart, matching my bleak inner landscape. But I kept talking.

"Of course, I doubt there are any publishers out there these days. Or agents. And I'm writing in longhand, with no reasonable expectation of publication, of anyone else reading it beyond a few friends. I'm not entirely sure why I'm still writing. I guess because it's a long and mostly delicious conversation with my beloved."

I took a gulp of tea, not sure what to say next. Was this an interview, to see if Sadie would let us stay? How could I convince her that a 79-year-old retired professor/bookseller and aspiring novelist could contribute something useful, maybe even meaningful, to her life?

"I'm not young," I said. "But I'm strong and healthy, and I love to cook. That was something Sarah and I had in common." I gestured toward the wood stove. "I'll learn to chop wood or grow food or whatever else you need. And I'm a pretty good storyteller." I looked around the cozy room, at the four of us gathered within the walls of bookshelves. I could open my heart to this woman, who held our future in her hands. If she let me, if she wanted me to.

We were silent for a few moments, until Miriam pointed at me. "Who are you?" she asked.

I leaned forward and took her hand. "My name is Jess. I used to live near your co-op."

Miriam pulled her hand back. "Do you know my Ben?"

I shook my head. "No. I'm sorry. I wish I did."

"He's in prison," Miriam whispered, then closed her eyes.

The dogs scratched at the door and Sadie let them in.

"What are their names?" I held my hands out to be sniffed.

Sadie pointed at the smaller one, one of those poodle mixes that were so popular a decade ago. "She's Big Mama. Her son is Little Guy."

"You mean the big one?" I laughed.

"Life rarely makes sense. Surely you've figured that out by now," Sadie said, touching Miriam's shoulder. "Come on, Miriam. Let's start some dinner to feed our guests."

Then she turned to Gloria and me. "Why don't you rest up a bit? You must be exhausted from your travels. And I bet you could use a shower."

A hot shower! I towel-dried my hair in our room, golden with the late afternoon sun. Gloria sat on the single bed under the window, tracing the squares of denim on the quilt with her finger. Drawings of dinosaurs and whales were taped to the wall over the bed, each one with Justice written across the bottom in childish letters.

"Do you suppose Justice is the child's name or a political statement?" Gloria asked, her expression contrasting the humor of her words. I tried to imagine losing such a budding artist. I couldn't look at the crib in the corner.


## Gloria

We ate at a long pine table, four old women huddled at one end. I tried to imagine the table full, conversation punctuated by the laughter of the children whose room we were borrowing. Maybe the baby would be in a highchair, face smeared with yogurt, and the young artist running around the table. We four were mostly quiet, other than "please pass the salt" or "this is so good." The lentil soup was delicious and the bread crusty. I reminded myself to eat slowly; gobbling food was part of my hungry life, especially when I was nervous. I wondered where Sadie got flour and how much dried beans and other staples she had managed to put away before the food supply chain broke down completely. The pandemic had made hoarders out of many of us, but we were still unprepared for life after the Undoing. Life with ghosts and not much else.

As if she read my thoughts, Sadie explained that they had goats and chickens and a big garden. Jeremy, whose bedroom we were borrowing, showed them how to use permaculture to maximize the growing potential of their land, and they had a large greenhouse out back. They taught themselves to put up vegetables and fruit and had a cellar lined with jars. Trained by the pandemic and then living so far from town, they had always bought in bulk, so they had ample stores of staples.

"Remember, we shopped for a much bigger group," she said. "Before."

The word and the bread both weighed heavy in my mouth. I thought about the people whose food I was eating and swallowed hard. This place sounded better and better to me, even as I became increasingly worried about the harm my presence might bring to Sadie's homestead.

"I need to explain something about myself," I said.

Sadie held up her hand to stop me. "Later," she said. "After washing up. I like keeping mealtimes calm. Safe."

Jess and I did the dishes and put away the leftovers. "This place is fantastic," Jess whispered. "Can you believe they have electricity? I guess it's lucky they're safely tucked away here, hidden deep in the woods."

I had trouble concentrating with her gushing. I had to decide how to be honest with Sadie about my situation without totally scaring her off. "Should I tell her everything?"

"Absolutely," Jess said. "She has the right to know."

"What if she tells us to leave?"

"Then we leave," Jess said. "But she should know, so she can decide. All we have left these days are our choices."

"That's all we ever had." I tried to laugh. "We just didn't know it then."

When the kitchen was spotless, Jess and I joined Miriam and Sadie in the living room. Sadie fed the wood stove. Miriam dozed in her recliner, Democracy on her lap and the dogs at her feet.

"She sleeps a lot," Sadie said, tilting her head toward Miriam.

"Dementia?" I asked.

Sadie nodded. Then she looked at me hard and pointed to the graphic on my "Fuck Patriarchy" sweatshirt. It's the one with the fallopian tubes ending in a middle finger salute on one side and a pistol on the other. Not that I've ever used a gun—or ever would—but it's a perfect metaphor for my fury. I couldn't help glancing at the shotgun leaning against the wall near the front door.

Sadie tilted her head and lifted her eyebrows in an unspoken question.

"You have a right to know about me," I said. "I'm a fugitive."

Sadie stiffened, as if she had been worried about something like this.

"I was a nurse. When my parents got sick, one after the other, I quit my job to care for them," I told her. "After they died, there was no money and I was homeless for a couple of years, until a friend helped me reinstate my nursing license, go back to school and become a nurse practitioner. I learned to manage medical abortions and perform extractions and got a job in a women's surgical center in Georgia. Great timing, right, with the pandemic and chaos in the reproductive health care system? Women still needed terminations, so we managed to stay open until the sexist bastards reversed Roe. That was a moment of truth. My clinic closed, of course. I threw myself into protests and lobbying and joined a Jane and Madame Restell collective."

Jess shot me a glance that said, *Do you really need to tell it all? She just met us.* Hearing my story, Jess must have questioned her lofty ideas about choices.

But I *did* need to tell it all. If I stayed at the farm, it could bring unwanted attention. Sadie needed to understand the risks.

"Madame who?" Sadie asked.

"Madame Restell helped women terminate unwanted pregnancies in the nineteenth century. A hundred years later, the Jane collective did similar work. Those two women are my heroes. After Dobbs, we came back with a strong underground network. We operated by word of mouth, set up secret labs, and made our own M&Ms. Misoprostol and mifepristone. After the election we increased our actions, targeting the right wing anti-choice leadership, picketing their homes and workplaces, sometimes causing property damage. Despite all our precautions and care, there was a mole—I still have no idea who—and the FBI focused on me. The collective asked me to leave town. I became a fugitive, wanted by the feds, and returned to Massachusetts to hide out. Since the Undoing, I don't know what's happening with my friends, with our work. If they're still looking for me."

"Or if there's still an FBI," Jess added.

"Wow," Sadie said. Did wow mean she was impressed?

Supportive? Or about to tell me to get back on my bike and cycle off into the sunset?

"You should know," Jess said, finding her courage again. "Gloria's on the terrorist watchlist. If there still is one."

"Terrorist?" Miriam opened her eyes. "Do you know my Ben?"

Sadie patted Miriam's hand. "No, they don't know Ben, Miriam. Let's get you ready for bed."

Sadie helped Miriam stand, then turned to me. Her face was hard to read. "Can they trace you here?"

"I don't think so. We were careful, left our useless phones back home, told no one our plans." Then I added, "It's easier to be off the grid when the grid is broken."

Sadie

It was surprisingly comfortable to sit by the wood stove with Jess and Gloria in the late evening chill, sipping warm goat milk to help us sleep. I grew cannabis, of course, and made a tincture, but it never worked as well as the old indica gummies from the dispensary. Miriam usually had no trouble falling asleep, but tonight she resisted, apparently upset by our visitors and the disruption to our routines. I sang her into slumber. As usual, it was "Ripple" that finally sent her down that simple highway to memories and dreams.

"So what are the good things about life after the Undoing?" I asked Jess and Gloria when I rejoined them, the lyrics of the song still scrolling through my brain.

It was a supremely dumb question, but I wanted, I needed, to talk about more general things. I had to sleep on Gloria's confession and the women's request. I hoped a good night's rest would clarify the decision I had to make.

"It almost feels like a betrayal to talk about positive stuff," Jess said, "in the face of so much loss."

"It's good to be positive," Gloria said. "I like that there's more time to think now. Riding bikes for so many days, you get into a rhythm, a kind of moving meditation. It's a huge change from the drama of my life those past few years. Working underground, always worried about being arrested." She shrugged. "But is that change positive? I'm not sure. I can't picture what comes next. Is there any possibility of something good?"

"I feel like I've been living in a shadowland since Gee died," Jess said. "When everything fell apart for the rest of the world, the basic needs of food and water and keeping safe became a kind of scaffolding, a structure, that keeps me from feeling the pain as sharply. Plus the writing, of course. Though that brings me back to the loss."

"I don't miss the technologies," Gloria said. "All the emphasis on virtual stuff, social media. Technology is a big part of what killed us."

"AI writing term papers!" Jess added. "I'm so glad I left teaching before that happened." She turned to Gloria. "Of course, if we'd had GPS, it would have been much easier to find this place."

I laughed. "Don't count on it. Even before, cell service was spotty here."

"I don't miss the culture wars either. Woke-bashing and book bans," Jess added.

"I like that there are no video games," Gloria added. "Traveling, we played a lot of cards and Bananagrams." She pointed to the stack of board games and puzzles on the low shelves under the front windows. "I love Catan. Maybe we can have a game?"

"Catan was my granddaughters' favorite," I said softly. "I'm not sure..."

"Or we could play something else." Jess looked at me. "So what about you? What's good?"

That was easy. "This place. The forest. Growing things and making things. Canning food and knitting sweaters. And in the past few weeks, as the weather got nicer, neighbors have started talking a little about sharing what we have, bartering for what we need. Miriam started teaching me how to paint with watercolors. I suck at it, but it's satisfying."

"I've always wanted to paint," Jess said. "Maybe she could teach me?"

I nodded, then said softly, "It might be a good thing David died in the tsunami, or at least I assume he did. Not having access to his insulin would have killed him more horribly. My granddaughter Rosie too. Without her inhalers...."

"Think about all the people dependent on big pharma for their lives. Insulin and heart meds and antibiotics. Not to mention eyeglasses and hearing aids and surgery," Gloria said.

"Surgery," I said, looking at Gloria. "That terrifies me. What if someone has appendicitis? Do nurse practitioners know how to do simple operations?"

Gloria shook her head. "I've observed common surgical procedures, but never done them. In the old days, I'd joke that we could just watch a YouTube video and try it."

I pointed at the bookshelves. "YouTube is gone forever, but Patty, who returned to civilization before the Undoing, was an NP and she left her reference books. I guess if we had to...."

Gloria shook her head. "This brave new world of ours isn't kind, is it?"

"Not kind at all," Jess said. "But there's a silver lining: our children can't put us in a nursing home against our will. There are no nursing homes left."

I looked at my lap. "No children left either."

Jess' face crumpled. "I'm so sorry, Sadie."

"On the other hand," I offered, "no more colonoscopies."

We were silent for a few moments, thinking about getting old without the safety net of medical care. Then I forged ahead. Was it too soon to ask this question? I needed to get to know these women, who might become what passed for family in the Undoing. The Undone.

"What's the worst part," I asked. "For you?"

The silence stretched for seconds that felt much longer. I wanted to say that the thing I missed most was being touched. But I wasn't that brave. So I tried to change the tone. "I miss coffee and real toilet paper. And digital photos of my family. And libraries."

Jess half-laughed. "Agreed. And streaming BritBox mysteries. Folk music."

"We have a turntable and some albums," I offered. "We can use a little electricity to play some tunes."

"And dance!" Jess said. "I haven't danced in years."

"What bothers me most," Gloria interrupted, "is that we couldn't stop the mix of lethal leadership and greed that brought us to this place. We should have fought harder. Should have done more. I guess we still have work to do. Once we figure out how."

I wiped my eyes. These women were going to be good for me.

## Jess

At breakfast the next morning, Sadie said we could stay. A trial month, to see how it worked out. There was a lot of work to do, she warned us, to grow and preserve enough food for the winter.

"Thank you," I said.

"We realize you're taking a chance with us," Gloria added. "We won't let you down."

We washed the dishes while Sadie and Miriam fed the animals and collected eggs. After Sadie set Miriam up at the table with her paints and small squares of paper, she showed us the basin where we could wash our road-filthy clothes. She gave us worn gardening gloves and shovels, pointed out where the garden needed prep work, and asked us to keep an eye on Miriam. Then she took an odd contraption from the shed. It looked like a cloth bag attached to a child's sled with large binder clips, pulled by a thick rope. Turns out that's exactly what it was.

"We're low on kindling," she told me. "This is how my grandchildren used to collect branches and twigs from the forest. It connects me to them, plus it's easier than carrying it all."

"Do you want one of us to come with you?" I asked. "Start getting to know the forest around here?"

"Not yet," Sadie said. "I need to check in with a neighbor, and I'm not quite ready for anyone else to know you two are here."

That worried me. How worried was Sadie about us, about Gloria, bringing trouble?

"No big deal," she said, reading my mind again. "Just being cautious."

Once our clean clothes were drying on the clothesline in bright sunshine, Gloria and I had a good time turning over the soil, getting it ready for the seedlings sprouting in the greenhouse. Miriam came out to join us, though she looked like she wasn't sure who we were. After an hour or so, I took her back into the house and admired her paintings, perfect tiny scenes of the trees rich with spring leaves, and the family portraits on the memory wall. Her work was more professional than I'd expected. I asked her to tell me about the people, but she ignored the request.

When Sadie returned, dragging the heavy sled-bag behind her, the three of us were reheating the leftover soup and setting the table.

"Most amazing thing," Sadie called from the doorway. "Let me wash my hands and I'll tell you about it."

Gathered at the end of the pine table over lunch, the four of us didn't feel as pathetic as the day before. I imagined, hoped, that having Gloria and me there banished Sadie's ghosts a bit. We chatted about the garden and repairing the deer fencing and Miriam's paintings and then Sadie sat back in her chair.

"So this thing is happening," she said. "Our closest neighbors, Madge and Gerry, are organizing a get-together next weekend. The first one. We've all been so isolated."

"We'll have to check our calendars," Gloria said.

Sadie laughed. A real laugh. I wondered how long it had been, and if our company helped.

"A potluck. Can you believe we haven't done anything like this since everything fell apart?"

Gloria and I smiled, wondering if we were invited.

"Of course, you'll come," Sadie said. The woman was a bit of a witch, or at least a mind reader. "And it's not only social. Madge has a plan for beginning to share our resources. Some neighbors want to increase their wheat crop and build a bigger grain mill. Start a bartering system, maybe coordinate security."

"What kind of security?" I asked.

"This is the first growing season since the Undoing. There are hungry people out there. Desperate people. We want to share, but not lose everything." She turned to Gloria. "You're the only health care provider for miles. You may become pretty busy."

That was both exciting and scary, but yes. Gloria could do that for this new home.

"That sounds great," she said. "Building a community."

## Sadie

As spring turned into summer, the four of us settled into a rhythm of work and comradeship. We three younger women, all in our mid to late 70s, got along well.

*Sometimes an Island*

I was less lonely than before Jess and Gloria came, but some days the losses still overwhelmed me, tides of grief pulling me down. Some days when it was too much to bear, I imagined that dementia might cushion sorrow and I envied Miriam. We all did, I think.

True to her promise, Jess learned to split logs and our woodpile grew. The garden flourished too, and I began to feel that maybe we wouldn't starve next winter. Gloria saw patients once a week on the front porch or in their homes and was studying medicinal herbs from books my science-teacher daughter-in-law Evelyn had shipped from Brooklyn. Our bodies grew stronger. We compared biceps, even held an arm-wrestling tournament one evening after enjoying brownies made with the new crop of buds.

Sometimes we shared snippets from our past lives, funny stories mostly. I never knew you could laugh and cry at the same time, but you can. Sometimes we talked about being old, about how we felt so much younger on the inside. Sometimes, late in the evenings, we tried to understand what had happened to our lives, which once-upon-a-time felt if not predictable, then at least contained by what had gone before. We never could have expected that in the late decades of our lives we'd be trying to understand a whole new situation. Trying to figure out who we are, as a people, when our society has fallen apart so profoundly.

Occasionally, events reminded us sharply of social disintegration and unrest. David's old shotgun was used more than once to deter those who wanted what we had. But our isolation, in combination with the shotgun and luck or magic, kept us safe. Our friendships grew, even though Jess was too curious—nosy, really. She often stared at my matryoshka dolls and the painting of the clay terrier, asking without words for their stories. I wasn't ready to share. I thought about bringing them into my bedroom, but I shouldn't have to do that in my own home, should I?

One morning toward the end of the trial month, I found myself alone in the house. Jess and Gloria had taken Miriam with them to milk the goats and gather eggs. I took the matryoshka dolls from the mantel and lined them up on the table, largest to smallest, left to right. They had been in my family for generations. My great-grandmother Deborah gave them to my mother for her sixteenth birthday and she passed them to her granddaughter, my niece Emma, on her sixteenth. I felt bad about my granddaughter Tillie being skipped over, but Emma asked me to safekeep them for her when she went to college. My mother claimed the dolls represented her nuclear family: father then mother then children in birth order. But when I researched the history of matryoshkas, I learned they were traditionally all female. The act of nesting them symbolizes fertility and childbirth, and I renamed them for the women of our extended family. My mother Esther was the largest, me next, followed by my daughter-in-law and three granddaughters, who have all been missing since that day.

"What do you think?" I asked the mother doll. She didn't answer. "I'm a bit worried about Gloria," I whispered to her. I had listened to Sarah's heartbreak about her beloved Ben, whose activism landed him in prison, leaving her so lonely. It worried me. Miriam and I could become collateral damage too if the feds tracked Gloria here. Was it worth the risk? I considered asking them to leave, but when I tried to picture how lonely I would feel without them, it felt worse than anything the FBI could do to me.

That got me thinking about Ben's prison, a cement fortress on the Maine coast. What damage would the tsunami have wrought? Could he have possibly escaped? And what would Ben think about the Undoing, the collapse of the grid and everything else? He had predicted this, from what Sarah told me. I tore my brain away from that ugly place and instead let myself play out one of my favorite scenarios, where he and Sarah outrun the waters and find a place to survive. Now, with spring, they are on their way home. Since my heart was writing this dream-story, they meet up with the others, with Jeremy and Zoe and the kids, with my son and his wife and my granddaughters. Any day now, they could arrive.

This hope that my lost family would return was a dying houseplant on the kitchen windowsill, barely alive, slowly withering into something desiccated that would disappear into dust if touched. Mostly, I didn't let myself dream those dreams.

Then one day something happened that made hope blossom. Madge and Gerry's son showed up, having walked from Worcester over several months. At our now-weekly potluck gathering, he told us how he and his friends hid out in their college dorm until warm weather, scrounging for food wherever they could, and then set off to their homes across ruined and empty towns, at the mercy of small groups of survivors.

"I had to stay away from the coast and riverbanks," he told us, his eyes wet and glistening as he talked. "The geography is different. It's all wrong." Then he would focus on the cornbread or chicken or fresh greens sauteed in garlic, making small noises of satisfaction after each bite. We all watched him eat, each of us feeding our lost people in our minds. Portland wasn't that different from Worcester, so if he could get home, maybe there was still hope for my people. That hope was better than alcohol and it triggered thoughts of other communal projects, like a lumber mill and maybe even a community center.

We all stayed later than usual that evening, basking in the unexpected joy in the room.

What happened the next day was my fault entirely.

Gloria and I returned home that afternoon later than usual. Neighbors took turns helping each other with the big jobs, and that day I helped rebuild a chicken coop for folks down the road while Gloria listened to the chest of their asthmatic daughter and made a makeshift splint for a teenage boy's broken finger. Taking off our boots at the back door, we heard laughter from inside and I felt a surge of gladness to have these women living with us.

Jess and Miriam sat at the pine table with the watercolors. My precious matryoshka dolls were spread across the table. Jess held the smallest, the one that didn't open, the one my mother thought of as her stillborn sister. Miriam was trying to put my oldest granddaughter, tetchy and adored, back together. I felt fury. Rage. Perhaps the strength of my reaction came from the emotion of the evening before, the miraculous reunion, and all it meant for those of us whose families had not returned. Or maybe I hadn't opened my home and my heart to these new women as much as I thought I had.

"No!" I screamed. "Don't touch those. They're mine."

Startled, Jess dropped the baby doll in the water jar. Miriam yelped and the two pieces she held tumbled onto the watercolor palette. Indanthrone Blue splashed onto Tillie's upper half; the lower portion bounced off the palette, rolled across the table, and fell to the floor with a crack. Democracy jumped off the table and dashed out of the room, knocking over the water jar.

I collapsed onto the floor, cradling the broken Tillie pieces in both hands. "You don't touch these. Ever!"

"How was I supposed to know that?" Jess asked. "If you don't tell us...."

"This is my house," I sobbed. "My things. My broken life. Not yours."

"I'm so sorry," Jess said. "I didn't know."

I shook my head hard, shoulders and arms and trunk whipping along. "Sorry isn't enough. Not even close."

"Fine." Jess stood up suddenly, knocking into the table. The water jar rolled to the floor and smashed into pieces. "We'll leave. Tomorrow."

It didn't end us, what happened, though it could have.

Once the moment of paralyzing fury passed, we each responded in our own way. I sobbed on the floor. It felt all mixed up, both the real lost family and the broken Russian doll which my mother gave to my niece, another lost loved one. Jess washed the paint off Tillie's face, dried it carefully, then led Miriam to her room for a nap, singing "Ripple" to help her fall asleep. Just the chorus over and over because that's all she knew.

Gloria sat on the floor with me, among the shards of glass and splashes of paint-tinted water, holding me while I wept. "Jess really better learn the words to that song," she said. That made me cry harder. Miriam's distraught interruptions from the next room calmed and then stopped.

We stayed like that until Jess returned. She started to join us on the floor, but Gloria stopped her. "If you get down, how will any of us get up?"

Getting up off the floor isn't graceful when you're pushing 80. We weren't ready to laugh at ourselves, but our mutual clumsiness moved us a bit closer. I sat in the rocking chair with Democracy on my lap. Gloria cleaned up the mess on the table and put away the paints. Jess found the tube of super glue in the kitchen gadget drawer and carefully fit the broken pieces of the matryoshka back together.

"If we had gold," Jess said, "I'd repair it by kintsugi, the way the Japanese do. They believe that damaged objects, especially important ones, are more beautiful."

I wasn't at all sure about that.

Jess and Gloria didn't leave. We weren't quite ready to apologize yet either, not in so many words, but we found ourselves being kinder. Touching each other more. Stopping to squeeze a shoulder, to offer a hand even when it wasn't really needed. Three days later, I brought my father's old typewriter into the living room and placed it on the pine table with a precious ream of paper. "You could use this to write your novel," I said to Jess.

One evening, about a week after the matryoshka incident, the three of us were reading in front of the wood stove after Miriam went to bed.

"I want to try to explain," I began, unsure of what I wanted to say, "about the nesting dolls and what happened."

"You don't need to," Jess said. "I screwed up, and I'm so sorry."

"I owe you both an explanation, even if I'm not sure I can articulate it."

Gloria reached over and squeezed my shoulder. "I'm listening."

"Those dolls are more than family heirlooms, you know? My great-grandmother Deborah brought them here from the old country when they fled the pogroms. The dolls are us, the old women, the crones, the unlikely survivors, caring for each other and building a new community. Mothering each other. These dolls are hope."

"And I broke one," Jess said.

"Then you repaired it," I said. "Now we move on."

And we did.

We started reading aloud to each other in the evenings, after dinner clean-up and the animals were fed. It started because Jess' eyes were failing and she missed reading her novels. But it turned out we all loved sitting around the fire and being read to. Miriam skipped her turns, of course, and Jess could only read a few paragraphs before she gave up. But Gloria or I read a chapter aloud, and then passed the book to each other, only stopping when Miriam's snores grew loud and the fire burned to coals.

# The Lost and Found Department
## the homestead · 2032 · Tillie

Annie had promised me that we'd visit the homestead right after the harvest and in time for Thanksgiving. But in late September, I started throwing up every morning. I'd been trying to get pregnant, the old fashioned, do-it-yourself way with a turkey baster and semen from Jake, one of the guys in our commune who was kind and willing to be a sperm donor dad. Deborah was born in April, a colicky baby. We couldn't imagine traveling with her as an infant, but on her first birthday, as we helped her blow out her candles, Annie and I decided to head to my grandparents' homestead as soon as it got warm enough to sleep in our covered wagon without freezing.

Yes, you heard me right. Covered wagons. Our horse farm collective had added plows and covered wagons to our offerings in this post-fossil fuel world. We used rip-stop fabric liberated from a shuttered L.L. Bean warehouse and Annie decorated them with abstract landscapes full of sunrises and rainbows, painting our hope that we might repair this broken planet of ours. Even with just word-of-mouth advertising, we could barely keep up with the orders.

Packing for the trip was challenging since we had little idea what traveling would be like, or how long we'd stay. Or what we'd find, though we didn't talk about that part much. My grandmother Sadie, if still alive, would be 78. Just your average geezer in the Before Times, but who knew in this brave new world?

I thought about Sadie a lot. She used to tell me that she believed we carry the trauma of our ancestors in our DNA, along with eye color and the ability to wiggle our ears. That means that my Deborah could contain genetic particles of the first Deborah's life, memories of burning houses and fleeing to safety. In my college biology class, I'd learned that it's a genetic swap, a two-way sharing of cells between pregnant woman and fetus. It's like we carry a genetic mosaic of our whole family tree inside us. I love this idea and have wanted to talk to Sadie about it.

Getting back to packing, Annie and I talked tentatively about staying at the homestead, if there was anything left there. Annie's Boston-based family was gone as far as we knew, and if any of my family survived, it felt important to be together. In the meantime, our work with the horses and wagons took most of our energy and Deborah sucked up whatever was left over. Annie did a series of sketches of the farm, the horses and the wagons, the gardens and Deborah's sperm-daddy Jake, so we'd have touchstones for memories if we didn't return.

We left in late May and the trip took forever. Most days we traveled 15 to 20 miles, so we were on the road for over two weeks. Deborah was teething for most of that time, but one of us had to stay awake at all times anyway, to keep watch, pistol near at hand. We had discovered early on that Annie's body could also make breast milk. We didn't have the hormones used for induced lactation in the Before days, but it still worked, so we could both feed our daughter, or at least provide a human pacifier for her sore gums. We had to stop traveling every few hours to get some exercise so we didn't go stir-crazy, and for the occasional campfire to cook. Deborah took her first steps on a grassy field on the edge of a river that thankfully had an intact bridge.

With so many hours of travel, Annie and I talked more in those two weeks than we had in years. We weren't used to free time, time not assigned to chores or necessities. Mostly, we reflected about what we'd lost, who we lost, and how we might build something new.

The light-bulb idea came to both of us at the same moment, the way it can happen when you are deeply connected to another person. We were riding along a potholed road one evening as we got close to the homestead, speaking softly so we wouldn't wake

Deborah, talking about life before the Undoing. About family gatherings and holiday celebrations, and how they felt flat and empty now.

"We need something new," Annie said. "A new holiday that means something in this new world."

I nodded, my throat too full of emotion to be able to speak. "A commemoration of the Undoing," I whispered. "On the anniversary in November."

"Yes!" Annie said. "We'll write our own Haggadah. Our history. Like for Passover Seders."

"To keep the memories strong," I added. "We'll tell about the Undoing and how it happened. All of it, the disintegrating ice cap and tsunamis and flooding, the earthquakes and destruction of the grid, the buckling of roads and tracks. The collapse of the world as we knew it."

"It will be an homage to everyone we lost, naming every family member, and conjuring their faces in our imaginations," Annie said, reaching over to wipe the tears from my cheeks.

As our horses clip-clopped up the gravel driveway to the homestead the next afternoon, I felt profound dislocation, like I was in two places at once. I was my adult self with my bashert and our daughter in a covered wagon, but I was also a terrified and furious 15-year-old in an ugly beast of a car with my sisters and parents, feeling kidnapped. My family were now likely all dead, which complicated any residual anger I felt toward them. Did you notice my use of "likely" there? Even now, three years after the Undoing, those of us who survived refuse to fully believe what the evidence suggests. But going up that gravel driveway I thought about the people who might be in the old farmhouse with the ugly new wing. If they were my people, they probably thought I was dead too.

The first person we saw at the homestead was my sister Eloise, sitting on the front porch. I thought she was a hallucination. El had been with the rest of my family in Portland on that day. She stared at our covered wagon drawn by two dusty horses and reached for the shotgun leaning against the clapboard wall.

"El, it's me. It's Tillie," I yelled. "Oh, El!"

Eloise dropped the shotgun and ran to me. We didn't try to talk, to explain, just held each other and sobbed. After a forever few minutes, I introduced her to Annie and Deborah and we all hugged and wept some more. Something was different about Eloise, something off, but there was no time to figure it out. Our voices brought an old woman onto the porch in a cloud of chicken and garlic and baking bread. It had been only three years since I last saw Sadie, but she had aged thirty. Her hair was snow white and she used a cane, but her gaze was bright and she dropped the cane to embrace me and Annie, who held our wide-eyed and for once silent daughter.

When we finally stopped hugging, Sadie reached for the leather strap around my neck and pulled the bisque terrier from between my breasts. She grinned at me and that brought more tears until Deborah grabbed the clay figure. "My doggie!"

If you've ever lost loved ones and then found them, you can probably imagine the disorienting mixture of love and joy and grief and regret, an almost unbearable stew of emotions. Over dinner, we met Gloria and Jess, friends of friends from Massachusetts, who had joined my grandmother and Miriam two years before. Miriam sat and ate with us, silently. Her eyes followed voices around the table but she did not speak.

"She'll be 90 soon," Sadie whispered to me. "She rarely talks but still paints. She's most herself with paintbrush in hand."

Across the table, Eloise sat next to Jeremy. The two of them were silent, curiously separated from the exuberance of reunion. They rarely looked at each other or shared a word other than "please pass the potatoes." Why were they so quiet? Did my arrival remind them too painfully of their loved ones who had not returned? El's twin Rosie? Our parents? Jeremy's Zoe and the babies? I wanted to know but their faces did not welcome questions.

"Don't ask," Sadie whispered, reading my mind. "Later."

That evening, I sat with my grandmother on the front porch, overlooking the meadows coming fuzzy-alive with green. After Annie brought Deborah to us for goodnight kisses and stopped to squeeze my shoulder, Sadie and I were comfortably silent. Listening to the peepers around the pond and enjoying the mild weather before black fly season, I felt like I'd come home.

"I'm so glad you're here," Sadie said after a while. "Will you stay?"

"We'd like to. If we can find a good way to contribute to the homestead."

"We need so much. And our little community is growing in numbers, as folks join us." Sadie took my hand. "Like you and Annie and Deborah. Maybe some of the others..." She didn't have to finish the sentence.

"So how many are we in the neighborhood?"

"Six farms. You know Madge and Gerry, just up the road. Their son and Madge's parents have moved in. You might remember the other neighbors, when you see them. In any case, you'll meet them at the next potluck. We're doing okay and we share what we have. Two other families have solar panels and one has a grain mill. About a dozen kids, though none as young as Deborah. By the way, I love that you named her that."

"After her great-great-great-great-grandmother. Have I got that right?"

Sadie nodded, her face serious. "It's hard to know how to keep our history alive when we've lost so many. Like the matryoshka dolls that Esther gave Emma. Now that Emma is probably gone, the dolls should go to you."

"They belong here, with all of us," I said.

"You came at the right time, Tillie. I'm not sure we could have managed the gardens and putting up enough food for next winter. Jess has been doing a lot of the food preparation and planting, but she's failing. I don't think she'll be with us much longer. Miriam keeps going strong, but of course she's not able to help much. Gloria is kept pretty busy seeing patients. There's no doc within miles, although Madge's dad is a vet. Sometimes he helps Gloria with her clinic. He says it's lucky that mammals have a lot in common."

"What's with Jeremy?" I asked. "And Eloise?"

Sadie sighed. "They've been here almost a year and I still don't understand. It's clear that they love each other but I don't know if they were together before That Day. I suspect they were, because they both seem to carry a lot of shame."

"What have they said?"

"Very little," Sadie said. "Something about Jeremy visiting the permaculture farm out near Worcester where Eloise was interning, and that's where they were when the tsunami hit."

"Zoe and the kids?"

"They were with your parents and Rosie. With her wheelchair, Zoe wouldn't have had a chance."

"He's so much older than El," I blurted. I couldn't say the uglier thoughts in my head, couldn't stop picturing Zoe and those sweet babies.

"She's 21. Jeremy is what, mid-thirties? Late thirties? It's not like there's much of a pool of possible partners these days, is there?"

*Life goes on,* I told myself. But I wished I had visited more often before That Day. I was so busy with Annie and the horse farm and our lives. I leaned over to kiss Sadie's cheek. "In any case, I'm so glad we're here. We'll talk tomorrow about how Annie and I can best contribute to this place."

Over the next few weeks, we three settled into the homestead rhythm. As Jess' health failed, Annie took over most of her jobs—chopping wood and helping Jeremy plant and maintain the garden. On the recliner—now frozen in a half-reclined position since the motor died—next to the fireplace, Jess joined us as we read aloud a couple of evenings a week. Gloria kept pretty busy seeing patients and the week before she had delivered the community's first baby, Madge's grandson. Eloise helped us with Deborah and did most of the food prep, with Sadie giving directions as needed. Since I was already caring for our horses, I added the goats and chickens to my other chores. It was spring and planting season. The work was demanding and never-ending, but being busy kept our bodies exhausted and our minds too tired to think.

The oddest thing was Miriam and Annie, who started painting together whenever they got the chance. Painting is usually a solitary art, but they stood together, each with a brush in hand, sometimes even working on the same small square of paper. When I asked Annie about it, she couldn't explain. "It just feels right," she said.

We all worked hard, but every day or two I tried to give myself a few minutes of alone time at the pond, in my favorite place. Not the flat rocks at the end of the path, but the mossy area a short walk past the reeds along the shore. I sat quietly with my clay doggie, remembering the early days at the homestead, when I thought he was my only friend in the world.

I brought my cup of tea to the pond one morning in late June and sat on the small stool I'd brought to keep my clothes dry in the damp moss. I caressed the terrier's broken tail, now worn smooth from years of rubbing. When I heard someone singing softly, coming in my direction, my first reaction was disappointment at losing my solitude.

Then I saw it was Eloise, and discomfort joined the party.

"May I join you?" Eloise asked. She waited for my nod, then sat at the edge of the reeds. We both faced the pond, watching the ducks who had become familiar members of the family, the new ducklings still fuzzy with baby down.

I tried to think of something to say. Eloise and I had not really talked in the six weeks since Annie and Deborah and I arrived. I admit I still wondered about her relationship, and it made me uneasy. When did I become a prude? I knew I'd have to let that go but it hadn't happened yet.

"I'm pregnant," she said. "I wanted you to be the first to know. Other than Jeremy, of course."

She giggled and the old familiar sound thawed my heart. I reached for her hand and squeezed it.

"I'm happy for you," I said, and was surprised that I meant it.

"I'm scared," Eloise admitted, still staring at the ducks. "No hospitals or midwives. What if something goes wrong?"

I squeezed her hand. "Gloria can safely deliver your baby, I'm sure."

Eloise turned to look at me then. "I want Mom. I want Rosie. How can I do this without them?"

We both wept then, still holding hands. Sitting two feet apart but beginning to mend.

It was Eloise who came up with the big plan, which she shared with us after dinner two weeks later. The eight of us sat around the outdoor fire pit, needing the smoke to keep the early mosquitoes at bay.

"We've been thinking," Eloise said, "Jeremy and me. The potlucks are great, but we need a community space, somewhere to gather with our neighbors. A place that belongs to all of us. We could bring all our books and make a library and have a food exchange, maybe even start a restaurant. Plus social stuff, you know. A place to make music and sing and tell stories together."

"Story?" Deborah murmured before returning to my breast.

"It was Eloise's idea." There was pride in Jeremy's voice. "We don't use all the rooms in the new wing. If we took down the wall between the two bedrooms at the end of the hall, I think it could be big enough. We still have lumber left over from the last project and our panels and batteries are working well."

"Space for canning parties and quilting bees and book groups," Jess spoke for the first time that evening. "I love it!"

Jeremy turned to me and Annie. "You folks were asking how you could contribute to the community. Maybe you'd be willing to head up creating a community center?"

Annie and I smiled at each other. This sounded like a project we could do together and love doing. We both had the same thought, about our Undoing commemoration somehow being part of this project. Annie explained the idea, her words rushing over each other in enthusiasm. "It'll be our story of survival and hope."

Everyone spoke at once, adding their thoughts and suggestions, until Eloise's voice broke into the excited talk.

"One more thing." Blushing, Eloise took Jeremy's hand. "Jeremy and I are expecting. And it would be fun to have a children's corner of the room, for them to play."

Eloise and I shared a quick smile as around the circle everyone burst into exclamations of congratulation.

"Before too long," Annie added, "we'll need a schoolroom. I think it's a terrific idea and I'm all in."

Gloria nodded vigorously. "It would be great to have a place to store health care supplies and maybe see patients a couple of mornings a week. I've started a remedy garden, following Evelyn's old herbal medicine books. They're pretty out of date, but then, so are we. So is this whole new world."

I stood up, cradling Deborah in my arms. "Time to put this munchkin to bed. I'm so excited about this plan. Thanks, Eloise and Jeremy."

It took us much longer than expected to get the space ready, but I thought it was worth the wait. And April was a good month for the celebration, before the intense work of the garden took over our days. Our plan had been to officially open our community space cum restaurant cum health clinic cum kids' space cum story room tomorrow morning with a community breakfast to celebrate Deborah's second birthday. Jess had passed two weeks before, so the event would also be a memorial gathering for our friend. An odd combination maybe, but it fit with the past three years of loss and renewal.

The night before opening day, Sadie and I sat together on the small porch, under the freshly painted sign welcoming folks to The Lost and Found Department. Underneath, Annie had added, "locally sourced food." A joke, of course. Since the Undoing, all food is locally sourced.

We ended up repurposing three bedrooms once used by the folks who moved with Jeremy and Miriam from Massachusetts but returned home before the Undoing. We kept one room separate, to be shared by the clinic, a classroom, and space for communal activities like canning garden produce and a clothing exchange. Jeremy and Annie had dragged a bulletin board and a blackboard from the old elementary school that collapsed after a quake. A white board would've been nice, but we could make our own chalk and who knows how to make those colored markers? Now the blackboard held a list of upcoming activities: a workshop on permaculture and one on knitting sweaters from wool recycled from unraveled sweaters.

The big room was the community area, with a kitchen area in one corner. We planned a breakfast restaurant three mornings a week and space for neighborhood meetings and our weekly potlucks. We had a bathroom, but the kitchen was the biggest challenge. Luckily, neighbors had extra appliances to share, and it turned out that Madge's son was a decent carpenter. The smell of fresh pine was welcoming and clean. The shelves near the kitchen held an eclectic mix of plates and mugs and serving dishes and utensils. No two plates matched, which pretty much echoed the aesthetic of our lives in 2033. Tables and an old sofa were arranged around a wood stove. Along the longest wall was the library, with all the books my mother shipped to the homestead ten years ago—oh, was I angry at her then! —and boxes from our neighbors. Our librarian neighbor brought books as well, saying that it was better for them to be read, since the public library was closed, maybe permanently. We found room for an old upright piano in the corner near the kitchen and a neighbor tuned it and donated a stack of yellowed music scores. A motley collection of guitars, banjos, even a psaltery, hung on the walls between ferns and walking iris plants. A children's table with crayons, paper, and homemade play dough nestled in one corner under a gallery of drawings and paintings. Another corner held a card table with a 1000-piece puzzle for anyone with a few minutes to spare.

My favorite part of the project was the frieze painted around the whole room, from about halfway up the walls to the ceiling, winding around the windows and doors. Miriam and Annie had painted portraits of our lost loved ones walking through artistic renditions of the landscapes where they lived and thrived, or had to leave: from a village in eastern Europe to an island in Penobscot Bay to a converted factory building in western Massachusetts to our homestead in rural Maine.

Expanding on the small images Miriam had painted in our home, the mural began in the early years of the twentieth century with the three young men and Jacob's 10-year-old daughter Deborah leaving the shtetl and settling on Saperstein Neck. The extended island families followed: Rufe and Esther and Mary and Caleb and Laura and all those zillions of cousins. The folks from the co-op were painted too—Sarah and Ben and Samuel and Patty and Rachel and Albie and Myesha. Perhaps some of them survived; we would probably never know, but they lived here with us now, in this mural that circled the new heart of our community. The hardest ones for me to look at were my parents and Rosie and Grandpa David. Hard, but also so beautiful. Portraits of our sweet Deborah and our newest member completed the circle. Eloise and Jeremy gave birth to baby Rosie in February, with Gloria's assistance. She was a healthy baby, who already had Eloise's calm presence. Finally, mostly for Sadie's benefit, Miriam and Annie painted images of the nesting dolls, each of them separately, and my broken-tailed bisque terrier; they were part of the family too.

I visited the mural every evening before bed. I kissed my finger and touched it to a few beloved faces, whispering goodnight. I often turned on the music for a few minutes, balancing the need to be frugal with our precious electricity with the desire to let my ghosts dance a bit. The music was on now, as Sadie and I sat quietly on the porch, and we listened to the faint notes of "Hallelujah," one of the ancestors' favorites.

"Who would have ever thunk it," Sadie said quietly. "That we would be able to rebuild a family. I wish my mother were here to share this with us."

"Esther would be proud of us," I said. I was proud of us.

There was so much left to do, to figure out. Bartering or a new currency, for example. And did we want to try to widen our community beyond the neighborhood or would that bring more danger and problems? And what about mail delivery? How would we handle it when critical things broke and couldn't be repaired? Most evenings Jeremy got on the old shortwave radio that Ben used to love and that Albie left for us when he returned to civilization. What if they found other small communities like ours?

"I wish Esther had agreed to come with us, but I knew she would never leave the island. And there's no way it could have survived the tsunami."

I did the math in my head. "She'd be 96 now."

"I wanted to spend those years with her," Sadie said.

All at once, the memories of that afternoon I spent with Esther the summer I was 16 came rushing back. The buzzing in the edge of my vision, how my skin tingled, my fingers were electric. And Esther, how she became Deborah, the first Deborah.

"Did she ever tell you," I began, but then hesitated, unsure of what words to use.

"About her time traveling?" Sadie finished my sentence.

"Whoa, you know about that?"

Sadie nodded. "It happened once when I was with her. Scared me to death. I thought she was having a seizure, or a stroke. Afterwards, she told me about becoming her grandmother Deborah, actually finding herself in Deborah's skin. How did you find out?"

"Same thing here," I said, remembering. "Except even weirder, it happened to me the same day. And I traveled to the future, to after the Undoing, and I was with Annie. I was 16, so I didn't know what to think. Never happened again."

She grinned at me. "I wouldn't mind seeing what life looks like ten years from now." Then her grin faded. "On second thought, maybe it's better not to know, huh?"

Maybe not. But when you have a child, the not-knowing is almost unbearable.

"Esther always said that some women in our line have strange abilities," Sadie said. "Seeing into the future, traveling there, *knowing* things. I think Rosie had it too. She used to talk about seeing ghosts, although Evelyn thought that might have been due to carbon dioxide buildup because of her asthma."

I hesitated. "Do you think it could have anything to do with our shared traumatized DNA? I don't understand how it works, but I can imagine our shared DNA memory-cells connecting us to pogroms and fleeing to safety. Now they're triggered again by current day suffering. Does this help us, or make it worse?"

Sadie shook her head. "I don't know, but I read that people with inherited trauma have lower cortisol levels, whatever that means."

I laughed. "This is one time when I wish my mom would lecture us about something from her biology classes, could explain how it works."

Sadie nodded. "I'd love an Evelyn-lecture right about now too."

I stood up. "On that note, it's bedtime."

Leaning on her cane, Sadie followed me inside. I turned off the music and stopped at the paintings of my parents. I kissed my index finger, and pressed it to Evelyn's forehead, then David's. I looked at Sadie, who was saying her own goodnight to her parents and then to Mary. "Goodnight, BFF," she whispered.

Sadie hugged me. "Big day tomorrow."

The next morning dawned as bright and clear as spring in northern New England can be. The scent of growing things, the earth moist and almost bouncy. Annie and I woke early. We deposited Deborah in bed with Jeremy and Eloise and their tiny Rosie and started the breakfast prep. By 8 a.m., The Lost and Found was full of people, warm and buzzing with energy. One activity led into the next: a buffet breakfast of scrambled eggs and fried potatoes and fresh greens, and then Madge at the piano leading us in a loud, if often off-key, singalong to Broadway musicals most of us had never seen on stage, followed by a vigorous kickball game outside. After lunch there was a break for naptime for the very young and very old, followed by Deborah's birthday party, complete with cake and candles.

After we enjoyed the buzz of precious sugar, we all wrote wishes for Deborah's happiness on small squares of paper and folded them into origami boats. We walked down to the pond and set them afloat, watching silently as they drifted. Deborah waved. "Bye bye, boats." Looking at the still water, we talked about the things we hoped for her life and the things she would probably never know, from cell phones to nuclear war. Silently, I wondered how we could do better making a world safe for the children this time around.

After a potluck dinner, we gathered around the stove in a circle of chairs and floor pillows to remember and honor Jess. We talked about her kindness and how much she adored baby Deborah. About how much she missed her wife, about her savory lentil soup, how her glasses always slid down her nose, how she typed away on that novel a little bit every day. Then Annie unveiled the portrait of Jess she and Miriam had painted on the wall mural and we all laughed. They didn't get her eyes quite right but she was flexing her arm to show off her biceps. I could hear Jess' voice saying, "Who knew an 82-year-old woman could make new muscle chopping wood?" We all blew kisses to Jess' new home on the mural.

Then we turned out the lights and lit candles. As her closest friend, Gloria chose the song and Madge played the piano. I put the bisque terrier next to the keyboard so he could hear us. We sang Jess off to the ghost lands, letting the final notes of "Sing me sweetly, Sing me down" fade into the spring night.

We were somber as we snuggled the little kids into sleeping bags and then rejoined the circle. Many conversations had led to this moment, to begin weaving our fractured past lives into a future. It felt like a necessity. A way to figure out who we were, without our old society. If our small world gets a second chance, who do we want to be? Our best chance to figure that out was by telling our stories.

Sadie started us off with a memory about the time Miriam broke one of the matryoshka dolls—the one Sadie insisted represented me—and it almost broke up the family. It hadn't been funny then, but she made us laugh and it felt good to laugh at ourselves. From there, the storytelling continued around the circle. Some offerings were memories, some fantastical, some pure longing, and some a mix of history and wishing. The stories embraced our ghosts and began to banish our demons. They all connected to somehow building a life in this rocky and wild and broken new world. Miriam listened intently, occasionally adding a word or two when it came around to her turn.

Our stories connect us and enlarge us. We are our stories.

Some characters in our stories are old and growing decrepit.

## Ellen Meeropol

Some are young and brand new. They are smart and resourceful. They are shattered and golden, grieving and joyful. They're born of our blood and our DNA, our trauma and our heroes. They are our worst and best selves. They are magical and all too mortal. They are our painful past and a slim hope for a future.

Our stories just might save us.

# Acknowledgments

I live in western Massachusetts, but my muse lives in Maine. When I started writing fiction over 25 years ago, it was on the island of Vinalhaven, in a cottage overlooking Hurricane Sound, rented for a two-month writing retreat. Now, above my writing desk hangs a large piece of paper with an elaborate family tree of the characters in the novels and stories I've set on my fictional version of the Fox Islands. I'm so grateful for that land and these dear, made-up people, who have hung around for over 25 years. I'm pleased to bring them together for an extended family reunion in this book.

Thank you to *Portland Monthly Magazine* and *Solstice Magazine* for publishing earlier versions of the stories "Sometimes an Island' and "Gridlock." My gratitude also to Paige's Place in Otis, MA, the inspiration for The Lost and Found Department.

Huge appreciation to my writing buddies and those who offered their expertise to help me get these stories right. Thank you, Lisa C. Taylor, JoeAnn Hart, Debra Immergut and the Fiction Kitchen, Jacqueline Sheehan, Maryanne Banks, Kari Ridge, Jennifer Jacobson, Mary Bisbee Beek, Perky Alsop and Michael Hoy. Special hugs to my amazing "deep dive" manuscript group — Julie Schlack, Liz Bedell, and Celia Jeffries. I'm deeply grateful to my writer friends Randy Susan Meyers, Patricia Lee Lewis, Celine Keating, Lydia Kann, Lesle Lewis, Jean P. Moore, my writing communities, and the independent bookstores that nurture and support our work, especially in these broken times. I'm so grateful to Meg Zaremba for the map drawing.

As always, special thanks to Straw Dog Writers Guild.

A big thank you to Mary Petiet and the team at Sea Crow Press; I'm so glad we found each other.

This is a book about climate catastrophe and personal loss. But it's also about the connections we forge with others, about the human capacity for hope and renewal, about leaving home and finding home, about the power of storytelling to point the way forward. We all have a lot of work to do, together.

As always, thanks to Robby, Jenn, Rachel, Josie, Abel, and Carol for the family love, support, and joy.

# About the Author

Ellen Meeropol, Photo Credit Jill Meyers

Ellen Meeropol is the author of the previous novels The Lost Women of Azalea Court, Her Sister's Tattoo, Kinship of Clover, On Hurricane Island, and House Arrest, and the play Gridlock. She is the guest editor for the anthology Dreams for a Broken World. Essay and story publications include Ms. Magazine, Lilith, The Writer Magazine, The Boston Globe, Solstice Magazine, Guernica, Lit Hub, and Mom Egg Review. Her work focuses on the lives of women, especially those on the fault lines between political activism and family, and has been a finalist for the Sarton Women's Prize, longlisted for the Massachusetts Book Award, and selected by the Women's National Book Association as a Great Group Reads. Ellen lives in western Massachusetts, where she is a founding mother of Straw Dog Writers Guild.

# About the Press

Sea Crow Press

Sea Crow Press is an independent, woman-owned publisher based on Cape Cod, where land meets sea and stories take root. We publish books that connect people to place, to planet, and to each other; stories that linger, provoke, inspire, or simply bring beauty into a reader's day.

We believe literature has the power to illuminate the climate era; not with fear, but with feeling. We champion work that entertains and endures, where emotional truth meets ecological awareness. Our books ask meaningful questions, spark wonder, and offer hope.

We are committed to amplifying underrepresented voices and building a sustainable literary future

www.ingramcontent.com/pod-product-compliance
Lightning Source LLC
LaVergne TN
LVHW032005070526
838202LV00058B/6303